I0667907

The Courier of Dunbar Gap

··

D.L. Barnes

Ocean Time Publishing LLC

Copyright © 2025 by D.L. Barnes

All rights reserved.

No part of this publication may be reproduced, distributed, or transmitted in any form or by any means, including photocopying, recording, or other electronic or mechanical methods, without the prior written permission of the publisher, except as permitted by U.S. copyright law. For permission requests, contact [include publisher/author contact info].

The story, all names, characters, and incidents portrayed in this production are fictitious. No identification with actual persons (living or deceased), places, buildings, and products is intended or should be inferred.

ISBN: 9798218702366 Paperback

Book Cover by Canva

First edition 2025

Dedication

This book is dedicated to the author's siblings, their families, and the countless healthcare workers who served selflessly caring for our beloved mother. At the grand age of ninety years old, our mother finished her chapter in this life to begin a glorious new chapter where she has found Love who was waiting all along.

Introduction

The Civil War was in its third year by the spring of 1864. It was a war that was to never last that long, and the toll it took ripped away at the heart of the democracy, founded less than one hundred years prior. General Grant had been to Knoxville and looked for options including using the Cumberland Gap as a passage to get supplies to the soldiers who would do the groundwork of invading the state of Georgia and shutting off its support of ammunition and supplies to Lee in Virginia. That option didn't look viable, and Grant returned to Nashville for a period. Grant would have to consider a different plan. In March 1864, Ulysses Grant took on a promotion to become the new Lieutenant General in charge of the Army's military operation. Grant's friend, William Tecumseh Sherman, took up the challenge and planned the invasion into Georgia. This story is a fictional story with characters that may not have ever existed, but if they had existed, what might they have seen or felt as approximately 100,000 Union troops under Sherman's command passed into the northwestern corner of Georgia. For the first time, Sherman had all three corps bearing down on an x on the map. General McPherson, Scofield, and Thomas were the three commanding officers at this point in time. Descriptions of the columns as they passed homes and villages included sights of men, horses, and wagons for four days in a row. Sherman left the ruins of Atlanta in the late summer, leaving a plethora of stories in his wake, some true and some just tales created by idle story tellers. Sherman sent General Thomas and the Army of the Tennessee westward. There they would eventually meet the Confederate forces near Franklin, Tennessee, outside Nashville. The haunting image of five Confederate generals' bodies laid out on a planter's home-turned-hospital porch is an image of the cost of war. Just as at Gettysburg, Kennesaw Mountain, Resaca, and Chickamauga, the war again claimed talented lives, never to be seen again. Sherman pushed his troops to the coast, ending in Savannah on what history is now known as the March to the Sea.

Geographically, the Appalachia Mountain chain starts in Alabama and travels on through the northern section of Georgia. The mountain range extends into Canada on the northern terminus. It is an ancient range of peeks and passes. Time has darkened the memory of the people and purposes of passages along its slopes. Wars and battlefields were present on these slopes since ancient times. The American Civil War brought soldiers along the same treks running towards or away from the enemy.

In the northern foothills of Georgia, people had divided loyalties in the war between the Union and the Confederacy. Not all supported the larger planters' interests, especially those who lived on family farms who grew crops for subsistence and not for cash crops that were made from the likes of acres set aside for sugar, cotton, and tobacco. In the remote lands where mountain tops and deep ravines existed, the mountains held a bountiful supply of secret hideouts, ancient passages, treacherous mountain roads, and a green canopy of foliage that hid strangers passing through. Locating gaps in the string of peeks were important pieces of information during Civil War times for both armies who did not always know the terrain. Sources reported that General Grant did that reconnaissance in the winter of 1864 to find the way into Georgia through the northern top of the state. Grant's promotion led to another general assuming that role, and General Tecumseh Sherman subsequently began his march through the state. He eventually reached the city where pirates and preachers once roamed. Their ghosts remain in the tales told even today in the city of Savannah.

This tale begins on highlands of Georgia, near the end of winter and the early spring 1864. Hear the rattling sounds of wind as it bends and twists the branches of the trees. When one hikes alone on the high saddles and through the gaps, one can feel a chill, but not necessarily from the breezy winds. One may begin to imagine unseen eyes following the steps of a lone traveler. Friend or foe one is never sure, but the heartbeat increases, and the pace becomes almost a run through the isolated wooded areas. Sometimes the traveler stops and laughs because it's only a furry squirrel scampering along the dried leaves, picking up nuts for storage. Other times, a genuine threat lurks behind a covering by a diamond head snake or a mama bear and her cubs.

By the time early spring arrives, the hardwoods pop with new life covering the mountainside, transferring the winter gray into a hue of soft limelight. The scenery is a painting created by nature. Larger rivers originate from trickling runoff or small streams fed by natural springs. The dancing waters on high cascade down the mountain sides to the valleys below, widening as more channels of water approach the larger stream of water like exits on a busy interstate. Creek bed trails are usually flat and more trafficked. The ancient paths run along the mountain, then dip and climb between peaks. The Courier of Dunbar Gap is a fictional story painted on the backdrop of the Civil War. It begins in one of the fictional gaps in the north Georgia mountains and ends by the sea. For the soldiers ordered to explore and protect Dunbar's Gap, it was a sanctuary from the direct fighting that was coming closer. Captain Hamilton felt exiled from his homeland and stripped of his gifts. It's the lowest time of his life, forgotten, lonely and lost without a purpose. From here, the ride begins.

Chapter 1

Dunbar Gap

It was before dawn, before the golden globe of sunlight hit the western side of Wilson's Mountain. Captain Hamilton was groggily aware of noises in the camp. Then the quietness of the darkest time of the night set in just before daybreak. He slumbered back to sleep for another hour of feeling warm enough in his covers. But not warm enough to face nature's calling. February still felt cold to a man of gentler upbringing, comforted with creature comforts like a bedwarmer. Gabe rolled off his pallet and put himself in the right frame of mind before he walked out of his tent. His assignment was to a recognizance group in the western division of the US Army, stationed with a group of men in a remote area of north Georgia to monitor activity through an Appalachian Mountain pass. The pass had no English name and appeared to be in the middle of nowhere.

Gabe estimated they were about to be about 4 days ride away from Chattanooga.

"Good morning, Hamilton," said one of the men he passed along the way.

Gabe just nodded and moved on. The captain kept his thoughts to himself around the men. The group consisted of primary teenagers, but also some older individuals with personal motivations for joining. Gabe was sure something was up to make him growl this loud this morning. The colonel's aid in camp was quick to come back with a cup of coffee and a pot filled with the hot brew on the way to the colonel.

"Here sir, take this quick. It appears the thief struck again last night. Belcher is beside himself, standing by the supply wagon. I need to get this over to the major. I'll tell you all I know when I get back." He hurried down to the cabin where Colonel Burton was sheltering.

"Sounds like no ham biscuits or breakfast or apple pie for supper tonight," Gabe mumbled and went on out to complete his morning walkabout camp. He noted where the food supplies had been until 8 hours ago and of the items not touched.

Mason returned with his effervesce mood and returned to the topic he had started when he had circled around with coffee. "No sir," answered the captain's questions. They seemed to have gone missing on the third watch. I didn't see any tracks. I'm not exactly sure how they done it. The thief took off the best smoked hams, some bags of flour. I'd say some canned goods were missing too. It's a dark place at night and the watch wouldn't see it the drop off through the growth of berry bushes and rhododendron down to the creek. Maybe they had a canoe. They might have been able to float it down the creek, but I would have thought a canoe would have been spotted."

"Maybe," Gabe replied as he scratched his stubble. He hated to go beyond a week without a shave, no matter what the other men did in camp. I suspect they knew their way around the area. Maybe there is some doing a little reconnaissance for the other team.

Mason chimed in, "Lee's up in Virginia, but they might have something moving this way."

Gabe stared off, sipped the coffee, and grimaced as he swallowed. He remained silent for a moment. There was no glory in war, even if you were on the righteous side. There was enough bad to go around in this war. "I wish they had taken the bags of coffee instead," Gabe quipped, breaking his silence.

"The colonel appeared to be to be deep in thought after the messenger arrived earlier this morning. He had barely come out of his tent than writing and reading documents and maps. He sent me to you."

"Okay, I'm on my way." Gabe said.

Gabe knocked on the cabin door and waited to hear the colonel's voice. "Good morning, sir," Gabe responded, to break the concentration of the colonel over the map that had been laid out across his desk. "Good morning, Hamilton!" The major continued to bore his eyes into the map on the table.

"I heard someone broke into the food supplies last night. The cook is all riled up about it. I'll send some men out to forage. There should be something in the area."

"Don't bother," the major said and then looked up. We are moving out."

"Really? So that is what the messenger was about this mor ning."Gabe showed no sign of emotion. He had been put here out of the way of Washington society intentionally. He knew his place was to accept and not to question.Gabe let his guard down for a moment to Colonel Burton, showing his respect for the man who ruled the hen house of this smoldering stew of men. "What's your impression of the horizon?"

"I suspect we are going to get a lot hotter if we join Sherman and his gang," said the colonel.

"I see. I've been watching the gray smoke. The sounds of rumbling thunder aren't from rain showers south of Chattanooga. I don't think it's all that stomping from church camp meetings either," added Captain Hamilton

The colonel nodded his head. "You are right about that. We are told to move out and be careful, as we will be crossing possible patches of the enemy. We'll stay close to the mountain passes as we head west. I don't have much faith in the Federal Road giving us much protection, so we'll travel along some roads and paths that give us better protection. We've spent the last six months jostling about in these highlands playing reconnaissance thanks to General Rosecan so we understand the paths that can get us from point A to point B. They may have guerilla fighters, but we have fighters with sense. There's no reason to put us in the valley for all to see until we need to dropdown."

"Yes sir, I suppose it would be safer with risks of falling on our backsides over a cliff down into a ravine than coming across a simple farmer who has a wife making apple pies for us to sample. Do you know there's a little town from a couple days' ride away from here that's named after a battle during the War with Mexico?"

Colonel Burton chuckled. "I can always count on you to give me the jaded perspective, Gabe. I can tell you that the little town you're speaking about has a little hospital there and you know what that means. I don't know where the confederates took over the home for their purposes, may be after Chickamauga. It's near the railroad lines. It's the enemy's means of getting things from Atlanta up to their troupes and northward. We know who needs those supplies badly. It's just a matter of time now before something is done about those supply lines. Our job is done here. The commanders found out something from our reports or information they are getting from other sources that's pushing for the next move. It's a beautiful piece of earth up here in the highlands and fine hunting grounds. I could see myself fishing for hours on some of these creeks. I would find myself a waterfall and take off all my clothes and cool myself to nature's finest. That's what I did when I was a kid in New York?"

"Grant does seem to be on the move and Sherman's knocking on Georgia's door. God's about to shake things up around here. I would agree with you that there is real beauty up here in the high country, but it's a hard way of making a life in the wilderness. There are no comforts like a good book and a hot apple brandy after dinner or a tavern to get a decent drink and I'm not meaning this poor excuse for coffee," Gabe responded.

"Hamilton, you surprise me sometimes. You make people believe you don't believe in a God."

Gabe made a grimaced. "I don't control what people think, and Idon't make people believe what I think. Church going or not, we all believe in something. Now trusting in that something is a whole different poker game."

"Sounds like the words of a man I used to be before I met my wife, Olivia," the major replied.

"I have no faith that a fluff of lace or silk would do much to change me."

"I suspect you're wrong there, Gabe. If you're still breathing,I suspect there's still time. Can't wait to get back to town where I can meetup with my Olivia. In the meantime, let's get the men together and break up camp. Once we are down in the foothills, we'll forage for supplies. We still have enough until we meet up with the medical Corp in Dalton. We leave in one hour."

"Yes, sir." Gabe walked back through the framed doorway of the cabin and saw the small sea of tents laid out in front of him. Trains were a much faster way to travel. But the men were still in the confederate held country. They were getting troops up and down the Mississippi now. However, the small division of men Gabriel came to know in the last six months would need to pick through the mountain passes and water crossings. The Southern Appalachians were a cover for soldiers, both gray and blue. Gabe accepted his new orders with cold emotions. What he thought was his world in the sophistication of Philadelphia and Washington was over. It was time to move out and write the next chapter of his life.

Two hours later, the men were marching near the foot of the mountains below the gap they had been protecting. The passage the men were on had once been part of a network of ancient trails. One of the traveled passes was to the east. Legend was that it had been a battlefield of two Indian tribes. Though not superstitious by nature, Gabe was glad the trail that his unit was descending from was west of that landmark. The pass was now behind them, along with the rough terrain of mountainous switchbacks and narrow passages. More substantial roads and open fields allowed the troops to move forward at a faster pace once they reached the foothills. However, they still found the dense trees along the less traveled paths provided better protection from the prying eyes of the enemy than the wider path of the Federal road. The group of Union soldiers saw a small village a short distance away.

Colonel Burton noted the grist mill along the stream they had been following. He patted the black mane of his horse as if the spirited stallion had led them to the treasure. The courier's information was correct. He looked carefully at the surroundings, looking for anything that might look like a hideout for the enemy, including uncooperative women or an old man who might take to carrying a skillet or rifle in their hands behind closed doors. It looked like a good spot to forage. He immediately had hopes that some supplies could be obtained here before moving closer to their destination. Colonel Burton sent a couple of men out to scout out the village ahead of soldier arrival in mass. When the scout returned saying it was clear, the unit advanced closer to the small oasis in the middle of the wilderness of the North Georgiamountains. Colonel Burton implemented his plan.

"Gabe, take twenty men and a wagon and move toward the mill.I'm going to march the men through town just to show that we're here. See if you can find some flour or cornmeal to replace that which was stolen. The ridge on the other side of that church will be where we all meet up. We'll load up the supplies and keep going on. No lingering from any of you, so move as fast as you can to forage some supplies and then move to the rendezvous."

"Yes, sir" Gabe picked out his men and moved out towards the grist mill. As the men got closer, there were signs of recent activity. All was quiet now, only the sound of the wind through the trees and the water flowing in blowing of leaves and the rushing of the water through the races as it powered the wheel of the mill.

"Hauss and Beams, look inside. Give us a signal if it looks clear inside. We'll come in and see what we can pack out once we get your signal," ordered the captain.

After a few minutes, both men can out and motioned the signal of all clear. As Captain Hamilton drew near. The men came out to greet him halfway. Sir, you're not going to believe this, but our stolen bags of flour and can goods are inside!"

"What did you say?" the captain responded with disbelief.

"It's all here as far as I can tell," said Hauss.

"What?" Captain Hamilton pondered the discovery and what it meant. "Amazing! Did you see anything else inside of significance?" Gabe asked.

"Just the inside of a mill. There are some bags of cornmeal and flour that aren't from our supplies. It looks like those are from some of the local people."

"I want to take a look." Gabe got off his horse and went inside the mill. He looked around and peered at something in the loft area. Take our sacks out and then burn the mill down. Looks like someone's been helping themselves with US Army Supplies." Gabe stood in place. He picked up a stick that was outside the mill and gave it to one of his men and barked, "light this."

"No!" cried out a high-pitched sound from above.

"You in the loft. Come down or I will burn this mill with you in it!" the captain roared.

"I can't come down," the voice responded.

"And why is that?" Gabe asked.

"I'm sick. I need to stay away from people."

"Is that right? Show yourself then." Gabe heard a rustling above. A figure came out of the shadows from above. *Frail in physical stature,* the captain thought. Gabe assessed that this spry could not cause too much trouble as long as the figure was alone. "Anybody else up there with you?"

The youth's head shook negatively.

"So how long have you been staying in the mill?"

"Just overnight, sir. I started feeling bad last night."

"Mm" Captain Hamilton motioned for one of his men to come near.He whispered something and the man left, bringing back a leather pouch and the captain's canteen.

"Child, get down here." Gabe then looked at the men. "You fellows, start loading the bags that are marked ours. I don't know where the hams might be, but look around. You might spot them in one of the smoke houses over there. We will retake our supplies and leave the rest alone. We mean no harm to the people who live here."

"Yes, sir," said the private, and the group of men started loading the wagon.

"You!" Gabe turned toward the slender youth. He noted the marked face with red dots. The cap hid the hair, and the clothes were of a farm boy's attire. "Now, child, come over here into the light. Tell me your name."

"I can't sir."

"And why not?" Captain Hamilton asked.

"It's not right, you are a stranger and I'm not to speak to strangers."

"Well, you've said enough already to break that rule. What's your name and don't play with me?"

"They call me Sam."

"Well, that's a start, Sam. Now come here and let me look at this stuff you've got all over your face."

"I told you I'm sick. I have measles. Leave me alone or you might catch it."

"I've had measles, so I won't get them. But I suspect you don't have them either. Ticks, jiggers, and head bugs might be a possibility though."Captain Hamilton rubbed a piece of soap onto a handkerchief and poured some water over the top. He then looked at the face of the youth. "How old are you?"

"I'm fourteen, sir."

"That's about right. Because if you were sixteen, you'd be old enough to be put in a Yankee prison for adults for steeling government property. If you were really only fourteen, I could say you were too young to be arrested for thievery. Now let me put this water on that feverish face of yours and see if those dots wash off. What did you use to make them?"

"Sir, I..."

"Stop!" boomed Captain Hamilton. "What did you use to make the dots?"

The youth quietly said, "I used beat juice, sir, with a bit of clay and water."

He looked into the youth's eyes and felt some relief, maybe even some sense of humor. "Well, at least that should all come off, eventually." He dabbed the cheeks of the one in front of him and sure enough, the stain was coming off. "Here, keep the soap and handkerchief and wash yourself off before it does stain that face of yours. I have a hankering to turn you over my knee, but I don't have the time or patience with a 14-year-old nymph who is into something weighs over her head."

Private James came back through the mill door. "We have it all and loaded up. Got the hams in from the next door. It seems like they have been using this as a storage center. No feed sacks with markings. I don't think they were taken from the confederates. Also, Colonel Burton sent a message that he's ready to pull out."

"Thanks, private. I suspect we are ready to go on here as well." Gabe stored the last piece of information in his head.

Sam's face lit up. "Sir, are going to meet up with General Sherman?"

"What does that mean to you?" Captain Hamilton responded back with suspicion in his voice.

"I'm told that the Army hires cooks and laundry women for camp help."

Gabe looked quizzically at her face without bearing his thoughts.

"I know two women who need the work. They are good workers and good women. They won't do what the paid women in taverns do, but they will do chores like wash clothes, cook meals, and do mending."

"Are you applying? I think not. I wouldn't have any valuable thing left in my tent." Gabe responded sarcastically.

"Not for me, sir! These women need their freedom, and they will be honest workers for real money so they can build a life and a future. If you can take them as far as General Sherman is, they can find work with the military. Further more, I didn't still your grub. I don't steal!"

Gabe looked blankly and paused for a few minutes, wrestling with something inside of himself. "How do you know where he is?" Gabe asked suspiciously.

"Sir, there is a war going on around us. I've been trying to avoid getting shot! I keep my eye on where his men are just in case their aim is bad."

"Sass, doesn't keep you too far from my pal here." Gab touched his horse whip. "I don't know where the man or his troops are moving. I've been up here fighting ticks and gnats for the last six months. Oh, just forget it!.I'm not taking you or anyone else along. You'd be too much trouble."

Sam stayed silent for a moment. "These women need prot ection.Anywhere, sir, where with the union column do. They will be safe there. You can help them."

"How do you know that? Do I look safe?" Captain retorted, losing patience with the delay of leaving.

"Sir, I believe your looks are deceiving because of the inability to groom and bath frequently in a civilized manner. Under- neath all that gruffness and whiskey-tinged breath is someone that is decent. I have faith that you were sent to escort these ladies safely behind the union lines."

Gabe said nothing at first. It would seem like this sprite had more information than what her five-foot frame contained. He looked at the pleading eyes and the fragile jawline. Gabe had

a memory flash through his head. That was another world far
away where enemies didn't lurk behind every corner. *Maybe my
friends were only illusions even then*, Gabe sarcastically thought.

The colonel had a gleam in his eye. "Seems like someone had
them waiting for us all along. Those two ladies there are under
your protection and will travel behind the cook's wagon.

"Sir, I didn't" Captain Hamilton protested.

"I suspect you didn't, but I have it on special request that
weare to escort these women to at least our destination. From
there, they mayplead their case to the commanding officer. At
this point in my career, I donot wish the displeasure of a certain
important gentleman in Washington."

"And who would that be, the one being pushed in or the one
booted out?" Captain Hamiltan replied.

"I take that as sarcasm and not disrespectful towards General
Grant or General Sherman. No, President Abe Lincoln receives
our gracious thanks for this one. I think you have heard of him.
Now let's move out. Put the ladies in their place in line. We need
to get rolling. We don't want to stay in the open like this, so
close to the confederates lines. I've made it alive this far and I'm
planning to make through till I'm old, very old. Now let's go!"

Captain turned and muttered some curses softly to himself.
He motioned for the wagon that was waiting on the knoll. It
was not the time to ask how he knew the ladies would be there
unless he wanted to be demoted rapidly. As the men took their
position and the wagons lined up, Captain Hamilton showed a
stoic face to the new companions. "You ladies must follow my

rules out here until we get to our destination. The men are not to give you any trouble or you come to me. You can share our grub, but I request that you separate yourselves at night so that there is no trouble until we get to where we are going. You are free to do as you wish after that."

"We will be fine, sir. We have our belongings and food to last us a week. The ladies and I will care for ourselves. We thank you for your protection, sir,while we are on the journey to our new home."

"Don't cross the men or I can't control what might pass your delicate ears."

"Yes, sir. We understand," the oldest women of the group responded. "We'll take that into consideration when thinking of what the best response for the situation would be."

"Good. That sounds like we have an understanding. Well, I'm not sure I have the jurisdiction of the cook, so you may be at his mercy. If he curses at you, that means he likes you. However, if he comes at you with a meat cleaver, I'd say he's having a bad day. Where's the youth?"

"Sir, it's just us. No one else is coming with us," said one woman.

"Why isn't the lad coming?" Captain Hamilton asked.

"Sir, there was no boy with us. You must be mistaken."

"I don't know what is going on here, but everyone seems to be in on what is happening but me," Captain Hamilton responded incredulously."

With that, Captain Hamilton rode up to the cook's wagon, said a few words, then went up to the front of the line. The signal was given, and the caravan was off to the west. Gabe's mind stirred with many thoughts, the least of which was the bewitching nymph with blue eyes and specked purple blotches over those porcelain cheeks. Gabe contemplated the danger that those eyes meant. *Move* on, *Gabe*, he told himself. *There's danger on the* path his *mind was taking. That was no lad in overalls. What was a female doing in farm boy* clothes *doing up here? Maybe she was some local brat causing mischief. But why would the colonel let the women* follow? *It makes no* sense, Captain Hamilton thought.

Day one uneventfully passed. The second day, intervals of cannon fire were heard along the journey coming from the west. The colonel stayed clear of the southern path that would have been easier to travel on and instead took a higher route to where he was going. By the third day the weather remained dry, The passage turned into little more than a cattle path through trees, ravines and sporadic cleared fields and white framed farms. Occasionally, laundry on clothes lines was seen. Some homes and cabins appeared abandoned creating a haunting feel through the landscape. Given that the tree leaves had not grown in layers to form a canopy, the path remained well lit, and the blue sky was a comforting sight that someone was watching over the caravan. It was in one of those moments that Captain Hamiltonwas jarred alert in his saddle. The colonel called a halt and shouted out to something ahead in the road. He called for two men in the front of the unit to go see what had caught his eye. The two men quickly moved forward about thirty yards and, after a few moments, gave an all-clear signal.

Colonel Burton requested that the captain come to the front of the column and advance to the gathering of the two other soldiers ahead in the path.

Gabe saw a young man dressed in union attire with his pant leg cut up to his thigh. A handmade splint placed along the length of his right leg indicated the nature of the wound. "What's your name, son?" The colonel asked.

"My name is John Martin, sir. I've been injured."

The colonel stayed on his horse but continued to speak with the young soldier. "I can see that. How did this happen?" Gabe asked.

"I was serving under the Ohio corps." We had a battle just a few miles from here a couple of days ago. I got lost. The confederates were still in the area, so I had to stay hidden. When I tried to get back to my unit, I fell. I tried to move on but eventually gave out. Eventually two people came by riding a horse, but I can't tell you from what direction. I couldn't see their faces as they covered their hats and bandanas. They told me a unit is coming. After helping me to this tree, they gave me some water and a little food and told me to wait here. They also said the band of US soldiers had a doctor who would look after my leg and get me to some place safe. I believed them. There was no one else to trust in this wilderness."

"I see." The colonel looked at his rear. "Captain Hamilton, can you assess this man's wounds?"

Captain Hamilton got off the back of Pepper and walked over to the injured man. "Let me look at the leg, John." After feeling the thigh and calf of the right leg, he replaced the splint. "That will work for now. With the colonel's permission, we'll put you in a wagon. When we stop for the night,I can wrap it and make the leg a bit more stable. I think it will heal in time if you can keep weight off it and keep it stabilized for a few weeks. You said there has been some fighting in the area?"

"Yes sir, three to five miles to the south and west of here.The confederates pulled out during the night from what I can tell. I tried to keep north of their line. "Thank you, John, for the information." The captain went back to his horse and talked with the colonel for a few minutes. He came back with a flask and held it up to the wounded soldier. "I think you're going to need this to help with the pain. Take a swig"

The young man looked up and reluctantly took the flask. "I'm not into drinking alcohol, sir. But I'm I don't think God would mind if I took some today. It's kind of like refusing His help."

"Son, you sure aren't looking at God, but I suspect if we found you in a place like this, he must be out there somewhere," the captain responded. The officer gave a signal, and the wagon wheels began to turn. *One more day in this wilderness and they would be grafted back into the large body of men of the Union forces. Captain Hamilton pondered what it all meant for his future. His face showed the men nothing of the tumult of emotions happening on the inside. Pepper received the firm tap by the rider's boots and the captain allowed the movement of his horse to* soothe *his anxious thoughts.* Later that night, when the troop had settled in, Captain Hamilton strolled back to the makeshift cot made for the soldier found in the woods today.

"Private Martin, how is the leg feeling now?" the captain asked.

"Its good sir." The young man answered. "If I don't move it or put weight on it, I can stand the pain."

"Seems like you were very lucky today. Can you tell me anything about the two strangers that stopped?"

"No sir, not really. They just found me laying in the brushes.Their faces were covered up to their eyes, so I couldn't see anything. They gave me food and water when they probably needed it themselves, but I took it anyway because I hadn't eaten in at least a day."

"How old are you, John?" Gabe asked, keeping the conversation flowing so that he could find out more of what had happened to this young man.

"I'm twenty-three, sir."

"Were the strangers about your size?" Captain Hamilton probed.

"Yes sir. I remember thinking that the one on my right could not hold me up by himself as he seemed so punny. Do you think you know who they were? The one seemed to know you."

Gabe took a big sigh. "Not sure. It sounds like our paths have crossed. You try to get some rest tonight. You'll be in better hands tomorrow." Gabe's mind was storing the information he heard. He suspected he knew where it was leading."

"Sir? Are you going to tell them how you found me?"

"Why do you ask?" Captain Hamilton responded.

"I was just thinking, that's all."

"What were you thinking about, son?"

John went silent and faked sleep.

Captain Hamilton stood in silence, not flinching from the spot.

John flickered one eyelid open and knew the captain hadn't left. He opened both eyes and reluctantly confessed. "Sir, I wasn't with my unit. I mean, I was, but I got scared. When they started shooting back at the hill, I knew I'd be going down if I didn't get out of there. I must have been near the end of the line because I kept moving left as we were pushing south. The next thing I knew, I was clear of the shooting, and I kept running. I never saw my unit after that. I was lost in the woods. There was a train track to my right. I figured the track would lead me somewhere if I kept it in eye shot. I knew we left some men in that last town we came from after the confederates moved out. I just kept walking north. It was getting dark, and I stumbled in one of the ravines. I tried to drag myself out of there and that's where they found me. That's where I gave up. I should have been left to die like in that field, some in my unit, some in the enemies. I don't deserve your help. I was found out there alive. I was the one to make the mistake of running. When my best friend Zeke made it across the creek we got separated. I kept telling him to follow me up the knoll. He wasn't following me anymore and just kept going.The one that found me and mended my leg told me to tell you the truth."

"I'm not your judge, but I thank you for telling me what happened."

"Would you have helped me if I was a confederate?" the young man asked.

"Yes, I believe I would have," Captain Hamilton responded.

"I was told you would say that," John mumbled. His face showed the strains of holding back his physical discomfort.

"Did the stranger say anything more?" the captain asked.

"Only a few things, nothing of significance for you. I was told you had a good heart." John turned his head away. "I'm still scared of what will happen next?"

"So am I, John. As for my heart, I lost it several months back. Now, I have an empty hole in that space." Gabe patted John's good leg. "Being scared doesn't make you a coward." The captain left the tent in silence. After that, he moved to his own tent for contemplation. It smelt like rain in the air, which was a change from the dry weather that had experienced the last several weeks. Spring brought rains. Soggy weather would slow down the wagons and chill the men as they made their final march to meet the column. Gabe moved his head to scan the environment. *What of the strangers that John met in the woods?*

Are they out there somewhere peering into camp? If they are on the same side, wouldn't they want to join efforts?

Chapter 2

The Camp

I n May 1864, four days from the start of the trip, Colonel
Burton's men and ladies had met up with the one corps under General McPherson. Colonel Burton had moved his small
group of men in 4 days from the isolated gap to a valley further south into the interior of the state, mysteriously avoiding
Confederate lines as the southern troops retreated southward.
The Union column had been on the move after traversing a
gap used to cross into the northern tip of the state. There had
been a fight a few days earlier near a place just south of where
they just crossed and came down from the mountain range that
separated Georgia and North Carolina. Gabe figured that the
boy with a broken leg had been a part of that engagement. Now
the confederates had retreated further south, most likely using
the river as a natural barrier. Sights and sounds of the Union

invasion are coming more frequently now. Gabe saw messen-
gers riding in the distance as the column got closer to the next
hamlet. The encroaching power of the Union Army was making
its presence known. One rider had brought a message to their
group. Colonel Burton read the message in private and only
shared a portion of it with his men. Colonel Burton seemed
to be inspired by the message's content. However, Gabe wasn't
sure that was the meaning of the colonel's lighter spirit.

On arrival, the women that Captain Hamilton had brought
disappeared. Gabe's only concern was that he followed his orders. Now the women were part of the commanding officer's
worries. Gabe suspected that the commanding officer had a lot
more on his mind than a small group of soldiers, a couple of
wagons of supplies, and two women in tow. For the next few
weeks there were some small skirmishes, but mostly the time was
to build up the supplies and rest the men before the big push
as the weather broke in the spring. The enemy kept moving
further south. It wouldn't be long before Union knocked on the
door of the factories and depots that supplied the confederate
Army. It didn't take a soldier's mind to know the importance
of controlling the city where the hub for supplies was located.
Gabe followed the directions when he entered camp and settled
with the others in his group.

Someone signaled Captain Hamilton into the commanding
officer's tent that evening. Gabe's first impressions were that he
was a fine officer. He was distinctive in style and spoke with
good diction. He was an educated man, and Gabe liked that.

The man had a warm, charismatic personality. Men came in all different assortments, and the Army was full of colorful mixes of people. Gabe had missed the comradery of men who had studied the classics and scientific practices as he met at college. This man, highly trained, was a soldier and a military leader. Dr. Hamilton's training to save lives and healing the sick seemed so different from the responsibility on this commander's shoulders? Yet, n*ow the two met on the same path. It was the irony of war,* Gabriel thought.

"Come in Captain Hamilton. I hope your treatment since you came to camp as been satisfactory!"

"Just fine, sir. I can see your men have done their share of fighting."

"Yes, they have." General McPherson gave a slight yawn. His eyes looked tired, but one could still see the softness of humanity upon his bearded face. "I am thinking you might like to be used more productively. I hear you are a surgeon."

"I accept my orders wherever the Army sends me." Gabriel instantly liked this gentleman and appreciated that he appeared to show an interest in what Gabe felt was his purpose.

"I was told as much by the authorities. My commander couldn't understand why the bears in the mountains needed better medical care than the soldiers fighting this war. Seems he had eyes and ears open when he was making his rounds looking for supply lines this winter. The general needs some doctors. You've been selected to be one of his finest when he takes back the country from the Confederates. Our mission was delayed by being pushed back to Chattanooga for a while, but we' are on the march again. It's all a travesty, if you ask me. Here we are fighting each other, sometimes even friends, till the death. The president wants the bloody war to end, as do the rest of us. There's been too much blood wasted. Washington needs a win for reelection. The country is tired of war." The general took a long drag on his cigar before continuing. "Anyway, I've got your orders here. You'll follow the medical corp for now. Major Steuben is in charge. He'll direct you to what you need to know. They are a good group of men. They like their whiskey, so remember when you need a favor. Don't tell anyone what you've seen here. By the way, they promoted you to major on special orders. You're being groomed to run one of the medical corps. That's the plan, Major Hamilton. They hurry things in this business when they need you. Also, the men are blocked out from the outside world. If some reporter reaches you asking questions, say nothing. Your job as a soldier is to protect your comrades. Do not release any information about our unit for any reason."

"Yes sir. I understand. Thank you for allowing me to move back into the role of a doctor."

"Someone's got your back, Hamilton. Here are your orders," said the general. Just then, a loud commotion was going on outside. It sounded like a feminine voice with a strong Irish dialect demanding to see the general. "Well, it looks like we have an emergency on our hands, so I best see what that is about."

"Yes sir," Gabe walked out of the General's office where he saw a woman with red hair in braids with fire in her eyes.

"Yes, madam? What can I help you with?" Gabe heard General McPherson say in a calming voice.

"General McPherson, I need to speak with you about an indecency of one of your soldiers."

"Sweet lady, what would have caused you such distress on this beautiful evening?" That was all Gabe could make out as he moved out of earshot from the commotion.

Gabe thought of his impression of the general. He thought the general to be a grand fellow with warmth in his voice and a twinkle in his eye. He would have enjoyed sharing a pint of ale and a few tall stories back in the pubs and clubs in Washington around a toasty fire. Yes, he would enjoy his company should they both make it through this war. Gabe walked towards his tent. *I'm being allowed back into my world again*; he thought to himself.

A tall lanky soldier that was part of Gabe's unit had stopped the captain on his way. The man asked if he would like to join some of the other men and play a round of cards after dinner.

"Thank you, Hauss. It seems like they are allowing me to play doctor again. I'd like to go over to the unit and introduce myself to the team first. It looks like I will be gone in the morning."

"Wow, so where are you going?"

Gabe held his tongue, remembering what the general had said. He spoke his words with careful selection, not to add information to his orders. "Wherever there is a wounded man, I guess. I need to do something things before tomorrow."

"Maybe they'll send a couple of us with you!" Hauss replied.

"I'll keep my eye out for you. Got to run."

"Good luck to you Dr. Gabe Hamilton! I'll find you after this thing is all over."

"You bet." Gabe made it to his tent. It wouldn't take long to prepare what was in his tent for the departure. He'd make one last pass by the stables to say goodbye to his horse, Pepper. Gabe had received him from after Manassas. The horse stayed around Gabe's camp that night. No one knew who the horse belonged to. The grayish white horse had pushed his nose into the ties of the temporary field hospital that was set up. Gabe just couldn't let him grieve alone, so he asked for the responsibility of the horse while he was in Washington. Gabe ended up adopting the horse that day. When Captain Hamilton traveled to Georgia after being reassigned, the proud and spirited horse came loyally. *Would Pepper come with him on his next assignment, or would they need to be separated from each other tomorrow?* The question was yet to be answered. Gabe contemplated being back in Virginia by the end of the month. It wouldn't be the comforts of home that he knew in Pennsylvania or back to the days of parties and fancy dresses worn by ladies twirling on his arm in Washington. Gabe felt his exile was ending. His purpose on the mountain passes of north Georgia remained hidden. However, Gabe felt the direction of the wind was changing, just like the color of the trees in the fall. He rubbed the whiskers from the growth on his chin over the past four days. It's time to move on and face what awaited him. After pleasantly enjoying a meal of potatoes and carrots in some type of stew with other officers, he walked around to a tent that was made into an infirmary. Supplies were already low, but sufficient to get them through a few more days. Major Hamilton helped where he could, and he was eager to check on some wounds and bandage wounds as needed. It had been months since he had done surgery, and he had hoped the Army would give him some time to acclimate back to his role as a surgeon. However, by midnight, he was back in the thick of what he once knew. Luckily, his skill set was still sharp, and he was carrying out his role as surgeon as if he had never been put on the shelf. He was lucky to have four wagons of medicines, supplies, and medical instruments. That followed the column in the field. He was fortunate to have such supplies as clean bandages, alcohol, and ingredients for a bromine treatment to prevent gangrene and ether. He knew that when the war began, a system was needed to support the troops. A classmate of Hamilton's from the medical college where Gabriel had studied was making great strides in creating a system for the east. A second classmate was working in the deeper south along the great river. He too was influencing changes to support the care for soldiers in the western campaign. Gabe had been stuck on a mountain watching the smoke of fires and dust from the columns as they moved. Except for a few snake bites that turned lethal and the common breakout of dysentery, Gabe felt his contributions to the war were rather slim and unimpressive.

When he recalled the faces of the men around the medical tent, his heart felt the suffering of the wounded. He also felt the need for compassion in all the chaos. Gabe was relieved around 2:00 AM so he could get some sleep before taking the train northward. He saw a gruff-looking lean fellow walking amongst the tents stopping and talking to some ordinary soldiers. Gabe tried to make out who the person was who moved so freely around the men. Someone had shared that the men passing through the ranks was General Sherman. His tall lean body gave him away. Some might say he looked a bit disheveled, but Gabriel knew it was a sign of battle worthiness to look this way among his men.

"I guess he can't sleep tonight, so he walked over from that farmhouse over there, where he's making camp for the night. General Sherman met up with us this evening. He's got four columns moving south now. I heard one officer say that it will take 4 days for all the columns to pass by a spot on the map if we go on foot. These folks are going to think the Roman Army is coming through," the soldier said before nodding his head and bidding Hamilton good night.

Hamilton just frowned but paid the respect back to the soldier. Gabe agreed with the thought. It was a morbid pageantry of men lined up in rows and columns to begin a march. The reality of life as a soldier at war was very different. Hamilton opened the flaps of his tent. The one next to Gabriel's was Dr. Mercer's. He was minding the watch over the wounded tonight. He reached for a canteen he had filled earlier with purified, but sadly, the canteen hadn't been. Too tired to take any further precautions, Gabriel took a big swig from the container. He then was ready to take out some toothpowder to brush his teeth, a luxury item sent in a care package by his Aunt Arline. He then heard some voices and footsteps outside the tent.

"Yes, General. Captain Hamilton's tent is right over here. I just passed him, so I know he's still up," Gabe did not recognize the voice.

Another voice stood outside the tent and spoke. "His title is now Major Hamilton now. Dr. Hamilton is fine for this evening. I signed received the paperwork my self soldier."

"Yes sir, my apologies. I meant no disrespect to the major."

"Dr. Hamilton, this is General Sherman. I would like to enter."

"Yes sir, of course." Gabriel stood in silence as he wondered what this visit was about.

"Thank you. Don't worry about formality this evening. I know you arrived earlier and have already been to the medical tent. How did it feel to be back with the knife again?"

"It was like I was back at medical school again, meaning I didn't know what I would see. I just tried to save a life." Dr. Hamilton responded.

"Yes, that's what we need. People skilled like you. General Grant and I have both had to face our fears and demons in this war. But we were ready to serve when called. The Army is calling you back to service in a highly needed area. You purpose is to lead a medical unit. I think General McPherson may have left that out of the bag earlier, but I want you to be ready. You'll get your first experience tomorrow on one of the newly created hospital trains. You'll be the general surgeon for the hospital train headed up to Chattanooga with wounded men. For now, you are under my authority as part of the division's medical Corp. You'll coordinate your services to support the medical teams in the area. Once you make a run on the hospital train, you'll be in contact with our commanding field team doctors. Major Coats will provide you with specific details. In the morning, one of the field doctors here will fill you in before you the train arrives. You'll get more information in the morning after you have some sleep. My aid will be around in the morning to give you your written orders. General Grant knows you're with us for now, but he's got his sights on Lee and it's going to be a bloody battle up there in Virginia. We need you Hamilton. I'm not embarrassed to say that. This is war. Men get hurt and sick. You are working for us in a highly specialized area, and we want you to know we think you can handle the role."

"Yes, sir," Hamilton replied with full alertness now.

"Also, I want you to know that you are advancement is being pushed through the ranks rapidly ."

"Thank you, sir. However, shouldn't I have proved my worth before such an advancement?" Hamilton asked, somewhat uncertain to question an officer higher in rank.

General Sherman quietly walked to the flaps of the tent. "You've shown your worth. For that, the Army is indebted to you. Good night, Doctor Hamilton." General Sherman walked outside the tent flap and walked over to the men formed around a small fire. Gabe watched as the man melted into the odd assortment of men he was conversing with on this cool spring night before sunset. The scene was General Sherman with his men in an intimate experience with his soldiers. War correspondents attempted but were never able to completely capture the full mystery of the bonding between the general and his men, though they tried. Major Hamilton looked at the general's face was haggard from the nights of restlessness and unkempt whiskers blanketing his jawline. In an extraordinary set of events, this man was selected for this role.

**

A two hours later in a framed house situated on the main street of a little village. The General stood up and lit a stick to light his cigar. "Sam, for God's sake, why are you still here? Why aren't you not home caring for some sick relative near a warm fire and a roof? This isn't the place you should be. Why didn't your brother send you back?"

"Sir. I was here because of my brother. I vowed to protect my family and do what I could to help those in need and assist in ending this awful war."

"I have said the same mission, but I'm not wearing petticoats and have pretty blue eyes. There is real danger that follows these camps, and I can't protect you from all of that."

"Sir, you let me bring your mail and supplies from home."

"That's different. Staff always protected you when you were on my errands, the same with the other generals. You were never out of our protection. This time you went too far."

"But sir, I had to find my brother and care for him"

The general touched his beard and paused for a moment. "Okay." He bristled at the thought that passed through his mind, but kept it to himself. "I received the message before you got here. I understand your commitment to family, but there are some people who will do me great harm if you are injured. I can't take that kind of responsibility. I have too much on my shoulders. You gave me gray hairs in this beard, and I already had them growing in when Grant left me with this whole circus. I guess he has his hands full enough." The General took a sip of his whiskey. He sat on the edge of his desk. I understand that you met up with Dr. Hamilton and your brother is being cared for."

"Yes sir. I had to leave him before the Corp came along the path, but I know they brought my brother with them."

"Yes, I know about that, too. I've made provisions for him to travel with the medical unit that's going on the northbound hospital train heading out in the morning."

Sam looked up with a start. "A hospital train?"

"Yes, they've converted some trains and are building some new ones that are meant to transport and care for men from the battlefield. I asked for some help, and this is what they are sending. Sam, I want you on that train too. You'll go in the officer's car. It's all written up in a letter for you to carry. I have some other correspondence in that pouch over there to take with you."

Sam went over and raised her eyebrow, asking if she could look in. "Is this to go too?"

Sherman nodded without saying a word.

Sam looked at the pouch for a second time. "I'll take care of it, sir." She paused for a moment, then broke the silence. "General Sherman, I have a question."

Sherman took another sip of his whiskey. "So I'm back to General Sherman when you speak with me in private, yes?" the general quipped.

Sam did not respond to the General's bate. "General, do you believe in God?" Sam asked.

"Now, if you're going to start a church service, go find another soldier. I'm not open to a camp meeting right now."

"But do you?" Sam looked up with tears rimming her eyes.

"Well, private, my wife does unquestionably. I am quiet on the subject when I speak to others."

"I know, sir. I respect your right to look after your own heart." Sam looked up squarely to look the general in the eye. "But do you hear Him when he has a message just for you? It's like when I bring you the mail. It's just for you."

Sherman pondered for a moment, but he knew Sam well enough that her question was coming from an innocent part of her heart. He saw that her heart was guileless and had not all the darkened by the cruelty of the world. His son had the same innocence. Sherman looked at the young women before him dressed in boy's military pants and homespun shirt. The waif melted the general's crusty heart and softened the weathered lines on his face. "Yes." He took a puff from his cigar and continued." I think I hear Him. I saw him in my little boy's eyes when he smiled, and I saw Him when he saved my life a few times on the battlefield," The general's face was grim, and he took another sip of his whiskey. He grimaced as the heat rolled down his throat. "If you need a deeper answer, I'll send you to General Howard's tent. He's more well read on the particulars of your questions."

Sam looked at the hardened soldier with tenderness. "I know he sees you even when you're downing the whiskey or smelling strongly of horseflesh."

Sherman felt the wetness growing around the lower rim of his eyes. "So that's the goal of this conversation. I smell a bit like flesh from the stables, and my breath has a hint of stale smoke and alcohol. You're growing up too fast, Sam. For that, I am putting you on the next train north. I won't be blamed for the mischief you could cause around here. There won't be too many trains coming for a while as I'm shutting off the valve to the outside. Now to another matter. Did you get to see your brother when he made it into camp?"

Sam nodded. She remained quiet, watching the continence of the general's face. Could she trust this man with her heart? When his columns leaves this place, he'll be in charge. Can he be trusted?

"Good. I am sending him away, too. He needs time to recover from his injury. Your brother can stay with the unit and the officer I am attaching him to while he recovers. We can let you meet up with your brother from time to time, bringing in the mail and supplies as you are directed. But only as you are directed. Got that! Take this pouch and go." Sherman reached down to a chest on the floor. "Your instructions are inside. There's a little note marked with a check that is to be given when you get to your stop near the last stop before changing trains. There should be someone there to meet you. If not, send me a telegraph from the train station. I'll have instructions."

"Yes, sir. Thank you, sir. How will they know me?" Sam questioned. She looked back at the general with the eyes of a doe.

For a moment he remembered being young, wearing a cadet uniform and dancing with all the pretty lasses. *Sometimes it was hard to recall what life was like before this war*, Sherman thought. He remembered, though. In the backs of his mind he remembered those innocent days too, if he could just return untarnished or at least less calloused, than he felt in recent months. "You'll know," he said. He turned away from the fire and took both of Sam's hands before she reached the door. "One last thing. I promise to be in church on Christmas Day in Savannah; if my wife's and your prayers keep me safe that far, I can at least pay Him a visit when I get there!"

"I'd kiss you on the cheek, sir, but it's the horse's flesh thing." She laughed and took back both hands. She swung around and headed for the door. "Oh by the way, if your keep your promise in Savannah, I'll know you're not the one they say you are. I have friends in Savannah, too."

The general took another puff of his cigar and exhaled with a twinkle in his eyes. "Go, private or I'll send you back where you belong. We never had this conversation, private." He took another long inhale and exhaled. He watched the courier leave the room. His thoughts disappeared into the vapors of smoke from the fire.

***

Through the night, Gabe tossed thoughts around in his head. Wherever he was going would not be the comforts of home, back to the days of parties and fancy dresses worn by ladies twirling on his arm in Washington. He had been in Washington long enough to taste the sweets of idle time on his hands. He barely remembered the smells and sights of dimly lit taverns near the docks. Gabriel vaguely remembered one such night when ale poured freely, and his money washed through his pockets because of the sly work of partners to the left and to the right. A crusty old sailor had come to his defense and challenged the table to double or nothing, as Gabe remembered through the fog of drink that night. It took three hands to send the table into chaos when the sailor exposed the plot of cheating at cards. Gabe at least made it to his barracks in one piece. His purpose in life had been a mystery through those early days in the military. Gabe felt exiled from Washington and into the wilderness because of a silly and jealous senator's wife. Women and their faults, Gabe dreamed, count them all like sheep in his head. However, his purpose still eluded him, hidden from him on the mountain passes of north Georgia. In his dream, Gabe felt the direction of the wind was changing just like the color of the trees in the autumn. He fell into a deep until the burst of the bugle woke him up from the darkness the next morning.

After taking care of the morning camp chores and washing up, Gabriel went to the officer's mess tent to grab a simple cupful of oatmeal and a cup of coffee. He grabbed an egg and put it in his pocket for later. There was a basket full of apples, so he took one of those as well and thought he would go down to the horse stable and share a half with Pepper.

Across the way there was a white framed church. Often these buildings were used to stable horses as the troops encamped in an area. This one seemed to be spared that fate for now. However, Gabe felt the church's very existence was in danger when bells rang for over five minutes just after 8:00 in the morning. The commotion formed around a group of people between the framed home and the church. It must be a brave man to call for church when the enemy is on one's front lawn and sharing breakfast while the restless are cleaning their shoes on with your wife's best white kitchen curtains. *It's a different kind of world when war arrives and a different kind of life one expects to live when the world is shaking."*

The women that Captain Hamilton had brought in the caravan of wagons disappeared into the camp. Now the women were part of the commanding officer's worries. Gabe suspected that General McPherson had mind was not on the small group of soldiers, a couple of wagons of supplies, and women in tow that rolled in from the gap. General McPherson was under pressure to lead his command across the river and head toward a town beside a mountain. From the top of that location, Sherman would see Atlanta for the first time on his march. This column would be the human ram rod through the heart of Georgia.

Chapter 3

Tracks

G abriel rubbed the whiskers from the four days of growth on his chin. As Sherman promised, an aid to the camp had delivered Major Hamilton a packet of written orders. After reviewing the pages, He walked around to the infirmary tent. Gabe was eager to check on some wounds. He was ready to take on his new role. Finally, about 2:00 in the afternoon, he stopped for a break and sipped some coffee. He was happy to taste the real stuff and not the counterfeit hot beverage flavored with hickory or sweet potatoes.

"Get yourself a cup, sir," said another soldier standing around the table set up for hot beverages. I just made a new brew. It should be hot.

"Thanks." Gabe looked up to catch the cook's name.

"I'm Gus. I have been following this Corp for almost two years. You're the doctor that came in yesterday. It's good to have you with us."

"Thanks. It's good to meet you Gus." Gabriel said as he filled up his cup.

"It looks like someone is looking for you." Gus nodded his head to the left.

"Major Hamilton, there you are," a young soldier said as he was rushing towards Dr. Hamilton. I tried to catch you and tell you that you have a box of provisions that someone left you for you personally. The general said to get some sleep. Someone will get you if you're needed between now and noon. We are already loading things on the train for a run up to Chattanooga. Equipment and animals first and then the patients so as not to keep them waiting on the train too long before taking off. We've got you in the middle hospital car. There will be two train aids and a general doctor in each of the other patient care cars. There is a medical staff car and a passenger car. Your horse will be in the animal car, and there will be a car that will have equipment, post, extra food and medicine supplies. Each of the patients has a water bottle, food supplies and a small kitchen and medical supplies. It's a newly designed train for medical relief. It's the one good idea that's come out of this war; shame that it took a slaughtering of men to put a good idea in action."

"Thank you, soldier." Let me get this coffee down and I will come over and look."

"Thank you, sir. We're glad you're with us. We have a fine group of men, sir. And our general, well, McPherson's got a place in all our hearts. He looks out for his men."

The half crescent shaped illumination in the sky seemed to follow Major Hamilton as he took each step closer to the depot. He spoke with some men he had known on top of the mountain. There was a stirring of movement as I heard the rumbling of a train coming closer in the distance. Gabe could see the markings of red and gold on the black shadow of what appeared to be a locomotive. It was a hospital train Gabe realized, but it was the first he had seen outside of Washington where it was being displayed like a parade float. It was a new idea that grew after the country experienced the early catastrophe in Manassas. Gabe recalled the wounded men lingering for hours, and sometimes days, in their own blood and agony before receiving attention and removal from the battle scene. Colonel Hamilton appreciated the innovation of converting training cars into mobile medical units. The new use of ambulances at the site of a battlefield was also an invention developed from the long, painful chaos of war. Medics could triage soldiers, sending the most seriously wounded by stretcher to a waiting hospital train. Colonel Hamilton would now oversee one of these hospital training courses. Gabe understood that this could mean a better chance of surviving. An awaiting medical crew could treat the men on the train. Now he was seeing this merciful beast with his own eyes.

Major Hamilton helped transfer the wounded and was the last one to enter the train car after the last wounded soldier was on board. He took one last look at the depot area and turned around to see the red lanterns hanging on the locomotive. It was time to care for the precious cargo that was traveling through the night. Gabe saw someone he knew in another car as he glimpsed through the window. John Martin had received his ticket on the northbound train, Gabe assumed. *Probably best for the soldier* anyway, *given he wouldn't be much use with that broken leg.* The next big town was only a few hours away by train.

Chapter 4

All Aboard

D
r. Hamilton was taking one last look at the leg wound
of a young soldier from Ohio. A horse had kicked him
hard in a field outside of Resaca when the beast got spooked
by cannon fire. Gabe was trying to save the leg by keeping the
wound clean from infection, but the wound was deep, and it
was hard to keep it sterile from all the germs in camp or at one
of the makeshift hospitals. This young man needed to be in a
cleaner, sanitized place if he had a chance of keeping the leg. He
told the nurse to bandage the leg with clean packing before he
looked out a window near the front of the train car. Fresh air
moved through the opening. Gabe could see that the train was
coming to some sort of civilization and suspected that he had
worked all the way until the hospital train hit Chattanooga. He
would try to wait inside as long as he could while the train was

making a stop and unloading the injured to a union hospital in the area. After that, he would go out to the depot. Another train was coming about an hour behind this train sent by General Sherman. This train would take him to Knoxville on a train with other military supplies and personnel. From there, he would leave the train and meet up with his new regiment. The train would restock and move to its next location. General Sherman had planned his supply with maps and data he had received regarding farms and supply resources along the way. Gabe was told that it took four days for all General McPherson's column to pass by a small town. He was sure it was a fearsome sight to those who remained in their homes when the mass of soldiers and war equipment passed. Gabe thought it was no different where he was going except that Virginia had felt the brutality of war for the last three years. Georgia was only beginning to feel the direct fire of an army that was larger and had more infrastructure to support a long engagement in battles. Did anyone really remember why the war started? Abe Lincoln said it was to free the slaves. Yes, that was a noble cause. Gabe just wasn't sure he felt any nobler after seeing young men die and women left with starving babies half frozen and malnourished because their husbands had gone to the battlefront. Some would never return. Was it like this in the wars of Rome when Cesar tried to conquer the world? Dr. Hamilton had nourished the spirit of cynicism while he was guarding the pass. Now his uprooted world seemed oddly exciting. Gabriel felt a glimmer of hope that something was about to change.

"Sir, your replacement has arrived. Dr. Gibbons will be back to meet you in just a few minutes."

"Thank you, Sargent Mills." Dr. Hamilton thanked the rest of the crew, looked around, and made a silent prayer for the men. He entered this war not as a particular religious man, but as time went on and the journey crossed dark places and painful experiences, he had grown silently reaching out to something in his soul. If there was an authentic place of peace, it wasn't out there. He needed to find it within.

An hour later, Dr. Hamilton was waiting at the train station with other officers and a group of reporters that were covering the war. Gabe remembered General McPherson's words and provided no information about where he had been or what he had seen since he left the mountain pass. The lights of a second train rolling into the train yard appeared in the dense fog. It was an eerie sight as the large black iron trojan horse-like figure pulled into the depot. A few shades raised on the hospital train once the locomotive came to a stop. Dr. Hamilton could see cars, bunks and the movement of oil lamps that were carried by the staff. Curtains blacked out some of the glow for the patients. For the soldiers, Gabe could only Imagen visualizing a mixed set of images through the gauze and cotton during the night runs. Other cars on the arriving train were dark and although there were people inside, the shades still drawn and there was little light t illuminating from the interior of the cabin. Since the train made it as planned, the railway was still open from where he came from, for how long Gabe was uncertain.

The conductor soon made his motions that those coming on board were to do so. Few came off at this spot. There was some activity around the other cars carrying cargo and livestock.

Gabe took a seat in the second car. A couple of other awaiting officers took seats near him, and they began cordial conversations while the train was being prepared to leave. It would be another four hours before they made it to Knoxville. Gave had loaded up on coffee and a ham biscuit. One nurse from the hospital train brought a small basket of apples and breads to snack on during the trip. Gabe appreciated the offer and put it under his chair on the train. After the first hour, he felt the need to stretch and excused himself from the congenial conversation with the other men. He walked to the front of the train and glanced outside through a blind that he moved slightly with his finger. The fog was still present but was lifting, allowing the countryside to be seen along the tracks. Mostly, trees were all he could see, but he could see light, and that gave him some pleasure. As he turned around in the car to walk back, he saw a diminutive figure in the back row of the train. Hunkered down, covered in a blanket, but noticeably shivering, was a young woman. Gabe thought about bringing the flask of hot tea that was given to him before the train departed. He grabbed it on his way back to visit with the person at the back of the train car. As he made it to the seat where the person was sitting, he noticed a person restlessly attempting to sleep. He took a quick glance at the face and shape of the person and boldly touched the face to check if there was a fever. With a touch, the person moved towards the light coming in from the corner of the shaded window, illuminating the face. "What the devil?" Gabe exclaimed as he observed the doe-like eyes open and stared back at him in fright. "You were shivering. I came back to see if you were ill. What on earth are you doing here?" Gabe said in a low tone.

"I'm leaving Georgia by train," the soft feminine voice said. The young women covered herself further by raising the blanket up to her chin, allowing Gabe to see her shivering hands.

"Here, sip this. It will help you get warm. Why are you on this train?" Gabe put the flask in her hands.

She drank a small sip and then another. "Thank you. That feels so good. I had special permission." She looked up at Gabe stoically.

"Is that the truth?" Gabe asked.

Sam nodded, but she said nothing.

Gabe backed off and wandered for a moment before asking his next question. "Are you hungry? I have some things up by my seat." He started to turn to get them.

"No please. I'm not hungry. I am just cold. I tried to dry my things by a fire before I left, but they didn't get completely dry, and it gave me a chill," she replied.

"Let me get you some more hot tea." Gabe walked to the front of the train where decanters of hot coffee and tea were available. He came back to the same spot at the back of the train. "Here you go. Try this."

"Thank you." Sam responded.

"Let's start anew. My name is Gabe Hamilton. What is yours?" Gabe pulled out his hand for her to shake.

"I'm called Sam by my acquaintances."

"I see, so we're back to that again, are we?" Gabe asked in sarcasm.

"I can't tell you my real name just now. Sam will have to do."

"Okay, Sam. So how did you end up on this train?"

"I've been staying near one of the small towns passed by the union troops. I was permitted a passage on the train as a favor of someone who was nearby."

"Most of the towns above where we started this morning are under Union control." Gabe responded. "You didn't come with our troops when we left the gap."

"No," Sam said as her jaw continued to shake from the cold.

Gabe treaded lightly with what he said next. "There's a lot of important people near the train station where we started."

"Yes," Sam responded. She looked away. "I suppose so."

"Can you tell me who helped you get passage?" Gabe asked.

"I wished to leave. My time here is no longer needed." Sam said. She pulled her coat closer to her body to keep her body heat in.

"I see. Are you going to tell me anything about how you got this far away from home?"

"Not now." She shook her head.

"Okay. Where is home, Sam?"

"I'm tired. Captain Hamilton."

"You keep secrets. I first find you in a loft of a mill in north Georgia. Does that make you a confederate? You are on a train with union officers, so what is your business here? Think carefully before you speak. Military prisons are closer than you think. With all those rats and crawling bug, I don't think it would be very warm either."

"Stop! You can't frighten me. Have me arrested. President Lincoln would free me himself! Here, have your tea back. I feel the company I'm keeping is giving me a bigger chill."

"Okay, I will stop for now." Gabe looked around to make sure no one was overhearing the conversation. "I want to know your story, but I'm a patient man. I think I deserve to know a little more about you since you keep turning up in my life lately."

"Yes, or maybe you keep showing up in my nightmare!" the young woman responded

"That may be true as well. He gave her the cup back. "You need this more than I do. I'm going to my seat so as not to raise talk. If we have another opportunity, I want to hear why you were in those mountains and why you are now on this train. I won't put you in danger, but I want to know. You put Martin in our trail. By the way, he rode up on my train to Chattanooga. He'll be almost as good as new, thanks to your attention."

"Thank you. I believe he is still with you. I don't think he left you in Chattanooga."

"Why do you say that?" Gabe asked, looking at her hands and realizing they were smooth except for a few recent scratches.

She shrugged her shoulders. "I saw him with your horse, Pepper. Not on him, of course. Pepper is in a car on this train. I think he was just checking on him and giving him rations between trains."

"Pepper is here on the train?" Gabe asked in incredulously.

"Someone felt the need to cover your back. That means someone in the Army likes you. Can't be me, so you have all 60,000 others under Sherman's command to choose from. Now, I would like to rest before the next stop. Please return to your seat and enjoy the company of those that would love to listen to your adventures or give their opinions on the most current events. I have neither the information nor the stamina to hold up much longer as a conversation partner."

Captain Hamilton stood silently. He then made a step back.

Sam quietly added, "Dr. Hamilton, I think you have a mark on your heart. Someone knows where you ride and where you lay your head. I would say you're very important to someone."

Gabe looked down for a moment. "I'm going back to my seat now. We'll talk more when we get off this train." Gabe wanted to process what she had just said. He thought he still might have time to figure out how to find out more about this muse from the mountain.

"Captain Hamilton, I did not steal from your camp."

"Now that is the most interesting thing I 've heard from you. Would you like to elaborate?"

"No. I said too much already," Sam replied.

"Well, I guess I should expect that from you," Gabe responded.

"I would like to rest, sir."

"Okay. I want to finish this conversation, though. I'll leave you to rest." Gabe went back to his seat for the next hour and did the same. He contemplated random thoughts rolling around in his head. They would be at the next stop soon. He hoped to get another opportunity to find out more information than.

Two hours later, the train came to a halt near Knoxville. Gabe at heard there had been some fighting in the area recently, but Longstreet and his men had gone back to flank General Lee. Gabe thought he would be asked to stay here when he first got the news that he would be transported to a medical unit. But apparently, his unit was only passing by. The train finally came to a stop. There was commotion as men got up to get their things from various storage compartments. Captain Hamilton took a glance at the back of the car and saw that she had vanished. The conductor was the only person standing at the back entrance. Gabe frowned. *So, this was how it would be, a mystery woman disappearing like angel dust. Convenient for me,* Gabe thought. He didn't believe in much anymore so what was gone no longer existed. He walked out of the train and was immediately stopped by the young man whose leg he attended on his way to meet McPherson's column.

"Sir, your horse and tack are waiting for you over there."

"What did you say" Gabe responded with disbelief as he acknowledged the young man with a salute back as was custom.

"Your horse, sir. Someone brought your horse on the train with the others. I followed orders, sir. It came from General McPherson himself before we left. I was made your assistant, sir."

"Son, you are supposed to be resting on that leg."

"I am sir, but I can still do things, and I was told you will need me. I am to ride in the wagon so I will not be hurting my leg. I am following the doctor's orders, sir," said the man they had found in the woods just a few days ago.

"If you're thinking I'm your doctor, I can release you of that burden immediately, but if that's the way it is to be, just point to where they are taking my horse, and I will get it. Tell me the Corp's encampment location so I can join them.

"Yes, sir. I believe they are waiting for you, sir, and a few others. There are a few wagons picking up supplies for the unit."

"How do you know all this, private?"

"Sir, they made me your assistant. I have orders too. However, I pick up the troop's signal while we were on the train. Apparently, they were awaiting the train's arrival. Perhaps there was something on board that was very important."

Gabe looked around. He sarcastically mumbled, "I see. Who are they?"

"My commanding officer-in-chief signed my orders. Now please sir, come this way."

Without questioning, he moved further down the ramp. Horses were being led to a staging area just past the road in a grassy area. Steps came closer and a male voice called out,

"Captain Hamilton!" A lieutenant from the 11th Corps came up to Gabe with a salute.

"Captain Hamilton, Lieutenant West here. I am to help you with your belongings and help you to our encampment. I have a wagon. We will put your things in the wagon. I believe your assistant will come with us."

"My assistant? Do you know about my assistant? Was that in your orders?" Captain Hamilton asked incredulously.

"Yes, sir. "Yes, sir. I believe someone will brief you upon your arrival at camp, sir."

Gabe felt more like Major Hamilton by the moment and less like the cast-off soldier on top of Burt's Mountain by the minute. What was happening? He looked at the men moving things on the train and pulling items off. It was an army of thousands moving in various directions, crossing the backwoods village west of the Appalachians. Something larger was happening than anything Colonel Hamilton had seen since or including Manasses. "Take these things and put them in the wagon. I'll find my horse and ride back with you if the mare is in fit shape."

"Yes, sir. I will keep the wagon where it is until you return with your horse."

"Captain Hamilton took a few more steps when he spotted something else from the corner of his eye. He glanced over without looking directly at the vision."

"Lieutenant West. Who's that man? Standing next to the carriage."

"Sir, that's Major Thaxton."

"I see. Who is Major Thaxton?"

"The man is an expert on building and dissembling tracks, along with some other things. He's one of the leading officers of the Army's engineering Corp. He can make things exciting really fast. Apparently, Sherman needed an excellent engineer with train experience, and Grant needed a talented surgeon. It kind of paints a picture, sir. Don't you think?"

"I understand Lieutenant. Who is the young women who is beside him?" Dr. Hamilton asked, trying not to show any interest.

"Not sure. They seem awfully close, though, so I suspect it is someone he knows very well. Yes, I don't wrap my arm around my aunt or mother like that if you get my message."

The Dr. Hamilotn moved his head away and mumbled, "Oh, crap!"

"What's that, sir?"

"Nothing Lieutenant. I think I better get my horse and get to camp so that the commanding officer can fill me in." Gabe looked in the couple's direction one more time. He saw her smile as she touched the Major's face. *I'm* cursed, Gabe thought. *The same reason I got sent to Burt's Mountain will be the same reason I am sent to the front lines.* I can't ever escape trouble when there's a woman around. Gabe made it to the staging area and stood by the fence. Pepper came out from the circle of other horses grazing and met Gabe at the fence with her nose nudging Gabe's hand. *"Lucky for* you, friend, *someone had given me a snack of carrots." Pepper eagerly nibbled the contents from Gabe's hand. He thought back. Gabe received a small bag of treats when he left Chattanooga. He thought one of the staff back at camp had left the snack for him before he left. Perhaps the nurse was in on the little* secret, *too. "There's seems to be a lot of secrets today, old friend," said Gabe and he patted the sorrel's nose. I know you're holding back on me too or you wouldn't be here." He affectionally rubbed the mane and neck of his horse and put the bridal and saddle in place.*

"Major Hamilton, sir?"

"Yes, that's me, and this is my horse."

"Yes, sir. A man with crutches just came by in a wagon and said you were coming. The wagon is just over there, sir."

"Thank you private. Do I need to sign something?"

"Yes, sir. The log is right here."

Captain Hamilton looked down in the recording book and noted Quintin Thaxton's name written above. His face turned to astonishment when he looked at the name above. Gabe scribbled his name beneath.

"Did Major Thaxton arrive today?"

"Yes, sir, about an hour ago. His train was on time. You can count on that. It will most likely be the only one that arrives on time."

Gabe smiled back, trying to be friendly. "And why is that?"

"No one messes with Thaxton and his trains if they want to keep their jobs."

"He's that mean?" Gabe lightly jabbed.

"He's that good, sir! Major Thaxton builds trains. He knows them inside and out."

"Thanks, private. Let me saddle up." Captain Hamilton mounted his horse, allowing questions to swirl in his mind. *Why would Thaxton know someone who was running around the* gap?

Chapter 5

Field Hospital

G abe had recently received another promotion, as foretold by General Sherman a few months ago. He was now carrying the title and duties of chief surgeon at a field hospital under the direct command of General Mead, but overshadowed by Grant himself. The fighting had been brutal during the most recent campaign and the casualties were mounting like ants gathering around spilled honey. Hamilton was making his last rounds for the evening. After saying some reassuring words to a soldier who had just lost his arm. He washed his hands and face before leaving the medical tents. Walking outside, he saw others milling around. He heard the moans of those in pain and wished he could do so much more, but he too had care for himself and find healing for his broken heart of the scenes of dying young men that he meant with every day. He felt a strange peace with it all, as if he had found his purpose. His hands gave back life to those who were sick and injured. The team felt a difference in the ward when he hung around. He didn't really understand it himself, except he knew he was giving something he didn't even know he had in him.

On this night, he walked over to his tent and took some cubes of sugar. He then walked over to where the stabled horses were. Pepper was eager to receive the gift. Gabe gave the thoroughbred another lump and rubbed his nose. "It's time to call it a night, but I wanted to be sure you got your treat for the day." The horse nuzzled Gabe's hand. The captain rubbed Pepper's neck one last time for the night and walked towards his tent. He poured himself a glass of water from the cover of the pitcher that he kept on his writing desk. Apparently, a package from home found him and was sitting on the chair at his desk. With his recent moves, it was difficult for his family to send him anything. The Army's chaplain and staff disciplined him enough to send a letter home at least once a week, usually on Sunday evenings after the church service. Gabe was glad the chaplain was a likable fellow who always brought a message of hope and faith. *These men had already seen* hell, Gabe thought. *An alternative to the life beyond what they had just gone through was much more palatable.* Gabriel opened the box sent by his Aunt Arline, who liked to send him warm knitted socks and embroidered handkerchiefs starched white and folded for his best suits. He didn't wear many suits these days, but he always found a good use for clean white cloth. There was always something edible in the silver tins. Sometimes a smoked ham or beef Jerky got through. Gabe liked to share the contents of the boxes with his comrades. He took a nibble from the fudge his mother had packed away and took out a book he kept in his travel bag. He started reading, when something fell from between the pages. A small patch of denim fell from the pages. He touched it and a slight smile lit up his face. Just then, his assistant came popping through the door.

"Sir, I am sorry to disturb you, but private Reynolds is delirious again and waking up the whole tent. A new casualty requires Dr. Fitz's immediate attention.

"It's alright, John. I will be right there. Get him ready and we'll see what's going on in that wound of his."

His assistant looked down for a moment at the cloth in the major's hand. He didn't say a word. He would let his commander have his moment. Sometimes souls meet even when the eye can't see the presence.

Gabe put the fabric back in the book. "I'm coming." The colonel got up and moved past the private on the way to the medical tent with the distressed patient. By the time he had reached the patient, two medics were holding the patient down. Gabriel quickly put a syringe of liquid into his buttocks and the patient yelled out for a few more moments. Within a few minutes, the patient was gently put back on his back. Dr. Hamilton sat with him for the next twenty minutes, looking over his stitches and wiping his brow. The man went to sleep and rested peacefully. This night he noted a star of David cross around the man's neck. He wondered if anyone had tried to get the foods that they would find acceptable based on his faith. He gave the nurse some instructions and left the tent again. Major Hamilton assured the nurses that he would check on him again in the morning.

When Gabe returned to his tent, his body was awake. He quickly undressed and fell on his cot. The sounds of cannons and gunfire, along with screams of injured men and clamoring sounds of the horse-drawn ambulances and wagons as they brought more wounded, filled his thoughts. Gabe tossed about on his cot. He felt the uncomfortableness of lying in his own skin, covered in perspiration like being wrapped in a putrid vat of grease. Gabe pushed himself back up to the side of the cot. He lit the lamp. He then pulled out the box that his mother had sent, digging out a tin that had some peppermints. His mother had printed a little prayer at the bottom of the can. May angels surround and protect you. Gabe took a sigh. *Where have the angels been the last six months*? He took a swig from his canteen. He felt something tingle when his lips hit the rim. Gabe remembered offering the canteen to a youth in a barn as he was heading out from the mountain town that guarded the gap. There was the soldier that was left on the trail and was now his aide. Sherman's main body then encountered him. Gabriel found himself on a hospital train bound for a battlefield to lead a medical unit. He had landed in that cold gap for the winter after being pushed out of Washington because of his flirtatious ways with an officer's daughter. Gabe realized he had changed over the past six months. He turned to deeper thoughts than the young, brash doctor he had been when he first signed up and went to Washington. Gabe emptied of something inside. Something new was being poured into the inside of his hard heart since he fell into the wilderness. It's what he needed to run a medical unit. He felt the tenderness of wanting to save lives. His new heart didn't want to be callous to the needs happening on the battlefield. Gabe stretched his legs and moved outside the tent. He looked up and appreciated the light of the stars above. *He silently prayed in silence. Help me desire your way and I will take that path even when I don't know where that goes.* Gabe rubbed his whiskers. He realized he had learned *to pray* again, *just like his mother had helped him to when he was a child before bed. The only difference now was that he prayed a little more throughout the day like when the sound of wagons came, the sound of cannon fire, or the sound of a screaming man when the medics moved him on the cold hard table for the surgeon to begin his work.*

The next morning, the sun's rays had not yet burst over the horizon, and an unusual increase in activity in the camp occurred. Gabriel opened his eyes and shook off the blanket to put on his uniform.

Private Martin called out to the Major before entering the tent. "Sir, General Grant is on his way. He has sent this message ahead of his arrival through a courier."

Gabe rubbed his eyes and put on his glasses. He opened the cylinder like container and pulled out the white envelope that was sealed with wax. He read the message and folded it back in the envelope and stuffed it inside the cylinder. *So we were getting a visit by the top general of the Army. The message said that the general would leave within the hour.* "We'll be ready. It's a good thing that he wants to see what's happening here firsthand. Hopefully, he will see something that will help him figure out how to end this darn war." The major started for the mess tent but ran into his aid again, who carried a fresh cup of coffee for him. Gabe thanked the young man and turned to look away. He caught a movement to the left of the stables. The movement was quick and galloping off down the path. It was still dark outside, and it was difficult to see the details of the rider or the horse.

"Don't be alarmed, sir." The private assured that was just the courier.

Major Hamilton walked over to the stables at a fast pace and sober expression. Several soldiers cleared an opening to let him pass. "Who was that?" he belted out as he got in earshot of the private at the stable gate?

Looking somewhat pale, the young man responded. "Who, sir?"

"That rider you just let out of the gate?"

"That was the courier sir." and the young man stood in straight posture, preparing to be addressed stiffly for not revealing more.

"I know that was the courier! Who was it? Saddle my horse, now?"

"Sir, the general of the entire U.S. military is coming."

Gabriel looked at the young man with narrowed eyes. "How do you know that, private?" he barked out.

"The courier, sir?"

"Did the courier tell you that?" Gabriel was thinking of insubordination and had a fire in his eyes.

"No sir," the Private Martin responded. "That was Grant's personal courier. Another soldier came with the courier and gave me supplies for Grant's horse. He told me the general would be here in the hour. He's standing post just a half mile down the road awaiting as a spotter." Just then, a signal observed through the trees and a man came out of the foliage and met up with a group of riders coming down the trail. Major Hamilton could see the commotion coming closer. Grant was on his way. He lost the opportunity to follow the courier. *Gabe would find her again. She's out there somewhere.*

"Private, when the courier comes again, keep her, no I mean him until you can get me!"

"Sir, I'm not sure I can. I have specific orders from General Grant not to delay or interrupt the duties of his courier. I'm not divulging any information to anyone. Grant signed the order himself."

Gabe looked down the road and saw the riders would be there in camp in minutes. As frustrated as he felt, he knew he had to stop the interrogation and return to the camp where people were waiting for him for directions. "Carry on private."

Major Hamilton spent the next two hours with General Grant while he toured the medical until. The short, unassuming man carried a powerful presence. He shook the staff's hands and picked out a chair beside some of the most intensively injured men. To Major Hamilton, it was like the General took the pain in himself and somehow energized him with a steel-like determination to get back to work and find and end to the suffering with no stops. At the end of the visit and the general expressed his gratitude for the work being done at the field hospital, he then made his way to his saddled horse."

Major Hamilton saw an opportunity to ask a burning question. "Sir, about the courier?"

"Grant looked down the path. "Major, I'm not aware of your question." General remained stoic and stroked his horse's neck.

"Yes sir," Major Hamilton responded. From that point on, Gabriel knew the courier was never to be disclosed.

Just then, Private Martin came from behind. "Sir, we have a patient asking for you. We can't keep him restrained and we are afraid he will break open his incisions if you don't come."

Grant nodded his head and tapped his cap. "Major Hamilton, take care of our boys. They are safe in your hands."

"Thank you, sir." With that, Major Hamilton turned away and walked back to a tent. He's purpose for now was service to the wounded lying behind the canvas. There was satisfaction in giving something to those who needed him for now.

After Grant's visit, several more months passed. The death of General McPherson hit Gabriel hard in September 1864. He remembered meeting the warm-hearted general in the spring.

"He was too good for this earth," the pastor said at the following Sunday service held by the chaplain embedded within Gabriel's Corp. The men and woman in the camp sang a hymn in remembrance of the fallen comrade. Gabriel honored the memory of meeting the General in person even if it had been only briefly. The young general left an impression on Gabriel that seemed to ward off the darkness of his own heart when the sounds and cries for mercy sunk into Gabriel's leather like skin. Somewhere, he could still hear the voice of the jovial commander responding to pleas from a feisty Irish woman defending her home against the rogues that were in every mass gathering of humanity. Even in war, one would hope for times of glimmering hope that the gift that transcends humanity was still there, never to forsake those who left wandering.

The courier didn't come that week or the next. The message from the telegraph from general Grant said the passing of General McPherson deeply saddened him. Sherman reportedly cried like a weeping widow. Gabe didn't doubt that rumor. Out there somewhere was a courier grieving too, Major Hamilton imagined. He could almost feel the grief when the night fell, and he tried to sleep. *We all have our way of grieving and celebrating the passage from this world to the next. Gabriel hoped he had honored the man who met him on the way from Dunbar Gap. The road wasn't clear then, but Gabriel knew he was* travelling in a new *direction in his life.*

Gabe carried on in the camp. He found a close-knit family of men and working with him dedicated to making the field hospital a place of healing and not a butchering table that others wanted to paint. Suffering was a description of war, but Gabe worked tirelessly along with other colleagues he had known since his medical training in Philadelphia to improve the delivery of care and sanitization so that more wounded soldiers survived. Gabriel had read about some work being done in creating skin graphs and reconstructive surgery to improve the disfigurements of soldiers that had recovered. That was an area that appealed to Gabriel very much and he hoped to follow up on this new area of surgery after the war. *Surely the war will end soon*. Some days, Dr. Hamilton felt 60 years old after hours of working in surgery and then making rounds. Both his hair and mustache were showing splashes of gray. He found sweet pleasures in the care boxes he received. Many supplies came in for the patients from churches and civic organizations. Boats came up the river to bring supplies from the north and outside the continental United States frequently now. Today, a schooner arrived and brought fresh supplies. The whole Corp was uplifted. A separate small chest came for Major Hamilton. He had forgotten about the simple pleasures of cinnamon and mint when he opened the chest the night of their arrival. He would ask the cook to put the spices to good use.

By Christmas, the courier had made a stop by the hospital. Grant had shared his best wishes and announced that Sherman had arrived in Savannah. Gabe went to the Christmas Eve service in the local town with several of the men from the unit. Major Hamilton was happy to return that night. The town's people had accepted their presence with open arms on this holiday, knowing these were soldiers from the Corp outside of the town's limits. The unit had a reputation of comforting the sick of all men, regardless of the uniform or race. It was the rule of the Major's, and no staff stayed who couldn't carry out those orders. Major Hamilton had promised the wounded men in the tents he would be with them on Christmas day. He even brought back a guitar that the pastor had given him, and he put it to good use after Christmas lunch. Once back in his tent. He picked up a cigar at the end of day and poured himself a glass of whiskey. Gabe brought it to his lips and then laid it back down. He poured the whiskey outside of his tent and went back inside to read a few pages from the black book. He would take a couple of hours to sleep and be back at work. Many surgeons spent the days in the field, spending the morning hours triaging the wounded on the fringes of the battlefield. At night, the surgeon's hands continued to be busy sawing and sewing flesh. It was a tale no one wanted to share, and many found comfort in opiates or alcohol from the mates who shared the misery. Gabriel sought comfort in his thoughts. In his mind, he could soothe the overburdened doctor he had become. He saw his family at the dining table talking about inventions and niceties that ladies brought up in conversations. The witty mannerisms he thought were just fluff then. Now those twists of words seemed like verbal jewels he wanted to store in his pocket just so he could take them out from time to time to admire the beauty. *What of the strangers that John met in the woods? Are they out there somewhere peering into camp? If they are on the same side, wouldn't they want to join* efforts? He often recalled the cool spring water flowing over rocks. There was pleasure in wiping the sweat from the brow with a wetted handkerchief from the spring in the gap. It was a matter of survival in those mountains, or one didn't leave still breathing. Gabriel also frequently let his mind question. *Where did she go? Was Sam her real name? Was she still hiding out in barns and hay, afraid of the danger of being caught?* These were the things he thought about after he eased his mind with the black book his aunt had sent him. His aunt had nine children and only three made it eighteen years of age. Gabriel understood the grief with each child's death. His uncle and aunt moistened the earth with tears with each fistful of earth they placed on each grave.

Aunt Arline would say, "The loss is painful, but the love within never really dies. It just moves on and meets us again somewhere."

Chapter 6

Surrender

It was late March 1865, and the war continued. Soldiers continued to fight and wounded numbers increased. The sheets continued to be stained with blood and the diseases continued to spread through the ranks. Sherman had moved on from Savannah after holding in place there for the winter and headed toward the South Carolina, whose fate would be like Georgia. North Carolina was spared much of the destruction that towns and cities had felt in Georgia and South Carolina. The end of the war was in the air.

In April 1865, an infantry unit stood outside a home near a small village on the road to Richmond. One private standing outside a redbrick home was from a small farm in Ohio. His grandfather had told him stories of the war against the British growing up. Those stories rolled through the private's mind, recalling his Grandfather Silas's tales of being at General Washington at Valley Forge. Had his grandfather felt the inspiring power from General Washington as this private felt about General Grant as he stood watch? A courier passed once or twice through camp this morning at high speed and would scurry back to the Grant's headquarters. The troops were on alert and fighting was still going on in the area. By afternoon, a small gathering was inside the house across the wagon path, including the Generals Grant and Lee. With intense expectation, the door finally opened and a general in gray walked down the stairs of the porch alone. The stiffness of his body except for the throbbing vein of his neck revealed the intense emotion the gray-haired general felt as he took each step to the bottom. He would walk through a column of soldiers from the opposing side. General Grant allowed the moment to sink in. There would be time for jubilation. Most of General Grant's staff had been a witness to the inside meeting inside including a member of an Indian tribe now a Union officer and a friend of Grant since the days before the Battle of Chattanooga. Grant's personal courier had left as soon as observing the signed surrender. As General Lee arose to walk through the front door, the courier fled out the back and on to the awaiting horse. It was an honor to bring this message to those who, too, had prayed for this moment. Tears flowed down the cheeks for several miles as the rider galloped through the forest.

In the field hospital some miles away, wounded soldiers continued to arrive in wagons and ambulances. Wounds from gunshots and cannon shrapnel were most of the injuries that Major Hamilton saw this late morning. The bloodied face of a young lad whose jaw shattered by a passing bullet was the last patient Major Hamilton has operated on this day. He did his best to sew the pieces of flesh back together. Would there be a way of getting this young man to a colleague of his who has the expertise of repairing faces of wounded soldiers? *Please stop the trail of* blood, *he prayed*. Gabriel had made the request each day since last Christmas when he started talking to the God he had read about in the black book. By the time the Major had finished checking on the last assigned tent, he was called by his assistant to come to his tent. A message was awaiting from General Grant, he was told. He hurriedly walked to his tent while Private Martin went off to the cook's tent. Major Hamilton picked up the leather pouch and looked at the contents inside. There was an eagle's feather inside. Hamilton turned and put his hands over his eyes and tears ran down his face with a huge, toothy smile. It's ending! It's finally ending, he cried out. Major Hamilton hurried to the tent, where the telegraph had further confirmation. He could share the news with the people at the hospital. Lee had surrendered, and it was only time before the rest of the southern Army would follow. Would Grant have known about the eagle feather and its meaning while he was at his post in the gap? *So few knew of the meaning,* Major Hamilton thought. Major Hamilton knew the word was getting out about the surrender. He searched out Private Martin to find the courier if they were still in camp. Gabriel would gather the staff and make a toast to a day they wouldn't forget.

"The courier has gone," Private Martin said when he returned 15 minutes later. "I'm sure the messenger left by now as the pouch was delivered."

"Why didn't you stop him?" Hamilton bellowed.

"I'm sure the rider would have stayed if he could, sir. But the courier has orders too."

"Was the courier identifiable?"

"I was not close enough to identify his face, sir."

"So you saw him?" Major Hamilton asked.

"Only from a distance, as the horse was galloping away. The hidden face of the rider never came clear."

"Did the courier see anyone here? Perhaps the courier picked up provisions from the cook or left a package for someone." Major Hamilton asked in exasperation.

"I can't say, sir. I did not see the courier while in the camp. I just saw the pouch and knew that was a sign of the courier."

"Wait a minute! It was the sign of the courier. Do not lie to me, Private Martin! Do you know the courier? Have you ever seen the courier before?"

Feeling pressure to speak the truth, the aide responded with an abridged answer. "I have seen the courier, but I have orders not to say any more. I'm not at liberty to provide any further information, sir. The orders come from a higher officer, sir. I have said too much already. Please don't ask me anything more, sir. Let's celebrate tonight! I promise to share a pint of ale with you."

"Private Martin, you're getting on my nerves. I have a hankering to request that you become a surgeon's assistant to another officer. More like a tall Scotsman, who uses a lot more colorful language than I do. Besides, you don't drink alcohol! I will repeat my question. What do you know?"

"Please sir, it's very important that I follow my orders. Have I not demonstrated loyalty to you?"

"Oh, just stop your humility script, private. When you act like that, it only brings the bad out to me. I might just get lickered up tonight and give old Dr. Cross Eye a piece of my mind."

"Yes sir, I think that would give us all some pleasure. Perhaps that might be just what you need to do to let off some steam," Private Martin replied.

"Yes, well it might, but I'm about 50 pounds lighter and would probably get my butt kicked to Kansas." Major Hamilton stood quietly for a few seconds and looked up again at the private somberly. "Has Sam been here Martin?"

Private Martin took a few more seconds to respond. "I believe we are talking about the same courier that has been with us since the gap, sir. I have never spoken of a particular name to you."

Gabriel soaked the response in, then smiled. "Thank you, Martin. We'll keep that information as a secret."

"Yes sir. Now I would really like to go back to the music. It makes me feel like taking nurse Molly's hand and twirling her around the fire. It's not a true celebration with fireworks, but the men will appreciate the end of fighting."

"You bet! I'll be joining you shortly." Major Hamilton walked back to his tent for a moment. He, too, felt the excitement of the surrender of the troops under General Lee. The end was an insight into this ghastly war. He was happy to be on the side who fought to end the oppression of others. He took a moment to celebrate by touching the soft edge of the eagle feather. He was told this day would come when he left the gap. An eagle's feather would be sent when his mission was done. He thought it strange at the time to be given such instructions, but the courier had left the packet of orders specifically for Captain Hamilton before pushing out. Gabriel wished the courier a safe ride. *May we see each other again* someday?

***

Several miles away, the courier bedded down for the night in a small barn near the river. *Thoughts swirled in her head.* I will *soon be able to put away these denim drawers for a petticoat and ribbons in my hair. Sam tossed in her bedding and her thoughts. "Come dance with me while the music is playing, and the stars light the night."* She felt herself sway to the rhythm of the wind. *Come back to the woods and the stream where we first met. May the eagle show you the way.* She was thinking of the songs and stories her mother had read to her as a child. Her mother had been part-native and part white. Her father had been a soldier and fell in love and protected her from the meanness of some people. While growing up, Lacey had spent time in the mountains and the valley's below. She also has spent time with her father's grandparents who raised her and her brother after her parent's death. She pretended she was warm and in her cozy bed snuggled under the warm quilt and a fireplace sending heat throughout the room. Sam imagined a cup of hot chocolate waiting for her as if she were home again.

The next few days did not magically end the war, but Sam had met the crossroads where she was now free to return home. The courier's pouch laid on the table of Grant's tent while he was out. Found in side the leather pouch was an eagle's feather. A note read. *At your recommendation, arrangements for me to sail home have been completed. I've been protected by the wings of an eagle.*

The headlines on April 15, 1865, reported the significant loss of another wounded casualty of the Civil War. Word of Abraham Lincoln's assassination reached the battlefield. Nothing could be done to save this man from the mortal wound he received. Major Hamilton walked through the beds of those men remaining in the field hospital. Most of them had heard the news already by the time he had made the rounds. He had allowed the doctor on duty to share with the staff the news that received over the telegraph. Like the death of General McPherson, the news hit hard into the stone walls of Gabriel's heart. Two men who gave off themselves. Killed by hatred. Deep soulish grief emerged for the loss and suffering caused by the war. It would be weeks before he ended his military connection. It will take a lifetime to process all that he learned from the experience.

Chapter 7

Meeting Major Thaxton

"**M**y enlistment contract is over. I have made my decision and don't wish to be persuaded. The Armory hospital will soon be closed here in Washington. I'm glad I was able to help these last few weeks once we moved all the men in the field hospital out, but my time in the Army is over," said Dr. Hamilton to his fellow soldier.

"I understand Major. I was to give you this for dinner tonight. This being your last night with us here in Washington, the group was hoping you would enjoy an evening with us, just dinner and some lagger."

"Well, I'm not sure I would be much company." Gabriel looked up again "You did say lagger, didn't you?"

"Sure, unless you want something else."

"No, a pint of that is fine. I think I would like to toast some-one properly this evening since I didn't get to make my goodbye when he left us." Gabriel broke the seal and read the card. "Yes, I will meet you for dinner at 6:30 in the lobby. I'm not sure if I know how to refine my beastly look here, but I'll try my best. It will make me do one more thing to prepare for civilization again."

"You are fine, just the way you are. You have half the nursing staff wanting to ride with you on the train tomorrow."

"Please don't tell them what train. I need to escape before one of them catches me."

"I promise. We'll get you on that train safely," Private Thaxton said with a laugh.

"Do you have all the arrangements for my horse, Pepper? I thought I was going to give her away once. Now I can't seem to part from the mare."

"Yes sir. It's all been arranged. Your horse will be well taken care of tonight and put on the train when it's time."

"Well, I guess you've taken good care of the old major all this time, Private Martin. I have appreciated having you along."

John's eyes began to tear up, but he stood at attention. "Yes, sir. It' been my pleasure."

The two men parted, and Gabriel was left to himself. He allowed the concierge to make a barber appointment in an hour. Gabriel sent a telegram to his family confirming his plans for departure tomorrow. He thought of looking in on an old friend of his in Philadelphia. He could spend the night at a hotel and ride the next day down to his family home some six miles away down on the Brandywine creek. Gabriel had the desire to ride Pepper out through the countryside and soak in the sounds and scents of what he grew up around. He smiled to think of his favorite pastry with raspberry jam filling. Aunt Arline made a tin full each Christmas. She would pour a cup of tea and grab the tin from the pie case and place it in front of him at the kitchen table whenever he came to visit as a boy. He had the best conversations at that table. After he went off to school, he returned to having tea in the front salon, as that is where young gentleman practiced their skills with charming the young ladies in the township. He must have spent a lot of time at his uncle and aunt's home as he became quite good at charming the ladies he thought to himself and chuckled. He missed those old days in the kitchen though.

A few hours later Gabriel had transformed himself into a clean-shaven fine specimen of an officer. He shared dinner and an enjoyable evening with men he had formed close ties with over the last three years. They all had become his extended family. There was a special time of remembrance for those that were no longer with them. The men including, Private Martin, held a tight bond for the colleague they were saying goodbye to this evening. The conversation was interesting, and the laughter was flowing.

"Well, look who just came in!" said one of the men at the table. "That's Major Thaxton. I haven't seen him in ages. I wonder if he's staying here at the hotel?" said Captain Myers.

"That is Interesting. He doesn't leave Grant's side very often these days. He spent some time with Sherman last summer. I guess everyone must sleep and eat sometime."

"He is a private man, but he's a good human being. I can vouch for that from what I've seen," chimed in one man at the time.

Gabriel's interest kicked in. "Do you think you could introduce me if he comes this way? I'd really like to meet him. I've heard a lot about him, but never had the chance to meet him."

"Sure," said Captain Myers. "Let me see if I can get his attention." Just then, Major Thaxton turned his face toward the direction of the men at Gabriel's table. Captain Myers gave him a wave and motion for him to come over. Had Gabriel been watching, he would have caught a slight twinkle in the eye of someone near him. He missed that clue, but remained increasingly intrigued by the figure coming toward the table.

Several seconds later, Major Thaxton had negotiated his way past the other tables in the room and was standing next to Gabriel. Captain Myers immediately made the introductions around the table.

"Max, how did we land in the same place at the same time?" the tall man said as he gave Captain Myers a firm handshake, followed by a hug.

"I don't know. We both must be staying out of trouble for a change. So, where have you been?"

"Mostly here in Virginia these last few months. I'm trying to help rebuild, although the stuff we worked so hard to tear up," Major Thaxton said with humor in his voice.

"I'm glad we have you up here for a while. I want to introduce you to some buddy. This is my good friend, Major Gabriel Hamilton. He's leaving us tomorrow to go home. We are out tonight celebrating his bliss and our loss."

"Hello, Major Hamilton" The man looked at Gabriel with a smile but said nothing more.

"I asked your friend to introduce us. I heard a lot about you. I believe we may have passed each other near Chattanooga. I was being re-stationed on the hospital train that went from Knoxville to Chattanooga and then on to Nashville."

"That's possible. I hope you have the opportunity to ride in one of the new cars that were designed. Those retrofitted cars were the best we could do for a while. I would appreciate your feedback on your experience using the brand-new transport the military is using for our wounded men. Thank you for all you've done. It is a gift to do what you do," said Major Thaxton. I've heard a lot of good things about what you did to help General Grant organize the medical units once you arrived."

Gabriel did not fail to notice that there was a gold band on the Major's hand. He still had questions about the encounter at the train station. Did being exiled to the lonely gap have anything to do with the mystery of his being recalled to an active life of medicine on the hospital train and then later to the hospital tents of Virginia? "I just tried my best to do what was needed."

"That's all any of us can do. We are all brothers, though. Never forget that," Major Thaxton added. He then bid the group goodbye.

The group of men at the table went back to their conversations. However, Major Hamilton watched Major Thaxton walk through the crowded restaurant. The officer did not appear to shy away from greeting several other guests present and he appeared to be in a cheerful mood. It became more interesting when a host swiftly met Thaxton on his way out and led him down the hall and out of sight. Apparently, he had another engagement for dinner this evening, one that was more private.

The evening ended with Gabriel walking himself back to his room. After several drinks after dinner, he could barely keep his eyes open. Tomorrow he would become a civilian again and go back to a life he had longed for these last several months. The train would take him back to Philadelphia and then Gabriel would follow his instincts. His family's home was a long day away by horseback from there. He thought he would break up the trip by visiting with one of his oldest friends and instructors from his college days who lived in the city. His old instructor would have some information about a post available or some lodgings that would suit his needs for the present. There were some options already offered , but Gabriel wasn't sure what his future would look like.

***

In another private dining area of the hotel, General Thaxton engaged himself in conversation with a group of men. It was a lively discussion of uses for steel in order to build the infrastructure of a nation that was expanding in the west and would need rebuilding in the south. The men were an array of friends, and colleagues, while others were practically strangers, but they all had brilliant minds. Thaxton was part of the inner circle coming from a family who had invested early in the manufacturing of trains and other equipment needed in an emerging industrial age. For a young man, he had ideas and the means to create new ventures. The war had only been a moral duty and soon this phase of his life would end. Quintin found most of the discussions this night inspiring, but he also had his mind on other things that he kept compartmentalized through the meal. Thaxton thought about his own plans for the future, which included further plans for later that night. Quintin had other plans for the evening. Meeting Dr. Hamilton was on the list of things he wanted to do, as his time was running out to cross paths with the doctor he had heard so much about. The going away part was a perfect idea for Quintin's purpose. This gave him another perfect alibi for being at the hotel at the right time. His luck was perfect. No one would know who paid the tab for the well-deserved going away party. No one had to know who Dr. Hamilton had protected these months. There was actually a small bit of jealousy tugging at Thaxton's heart after he met the man close up. But Quintin was of strong enough stock to brush those feelings away. He saw in the young doctor a likable gentleman with good looks and charm. Quintin could understand how that would get him into trouble coming to a quagmire like Washington, where power was everything and temptations abound everywhere. Major Thaxton cut the evening short after dinner. He politely excused himself shortly after the men were requesting after-dinner drinks around 8:30PM. Quintin quietly walked up to the 5th floor of the hotel. He found the unmarked door and Thaxton turned the key to let himself in. A whiff of fragrance permeated the room and the Major Thaxton was relieved to see the vision he had kept in his thoughts since he left Washington over a year ago. Major Thaxton spent the rest of the evening and into the early morning hours devoted to listening to stories from the military courier ending her last mission. Tales of the recent adventures were to be forgotten by morning, not to be repeated. The conversation never happened according to the participant's memory several months later. The tales simply vanished. When the staff came to clean the room the next morning, both occupants had left. The scent of lilac and rosewater lingered. Quintin left knowing the one. person that mattered in this world still believed in him in spite of the horrors of war.

Chapter 8

Citizen Hamilton

Major Hamilton was now a citizen again. His title of Dr. Hamilton was not totally new, but it showed a shift in how he saw himself. Arriving in Philadelphia, he had personal business to address. The plan was that he would stay at a boarding house near the college. This would allow him to reconnect to something he had left three years ago. On the fourth day of his stay, he planned to visit an old instructor. His home was on Dogwood Avenue, a pleasant residential area lined with a row of brownstone home on either side of the street near the college. It was a convenient walk from the boarding house that Gabriel had picked out for the week.

Professor Stockton had lost much hair upon the crown of his head, but his face was till as round, and his voice was cheery as it always had been. "Gabriel, how splendid you should call on me. I enjoyed reading about your adventures in your letters and am most impressed. The messenger gave me quite a thrill when I saw your card. Major in the Army? That's impressive."

"It's just a title. I'm sure I made it all seem grandiose. In reality, there was a lot of ordinary routine packed into months of being in the military."

"That may be true, but even the ordinary can be interesting when it you are away from the comforts of one's home. I insist that you stay here tonight. I will let my housekeeper get your things from the lodging house you reserved. I have a comfortable brownstone here, just a bachelor's pad really, but you have your own room and a privy that's yours alone. This gout has me uncomfortable at best right now, but an evening talking with you will keep me distracted from this infliction. Let me pour you something. A little brandy or perhaps a scotch would be do nicely."

"Thank you, whatever is your preference." Both men sat and chatted for briefly over a quarter of an hour. Then, sounds of a commotion at the front alerted both men in the library. Someone had arrived at the entrance. A few seconds later, the housekeeper opened the library door and closed it softly behind her. She brought a message to the professor.

Dr. Stockton looked very somber as he read the note. He looked up at Gabriel. "One of my neighbors has requested my presence for a medical emergency. Apparently, someone in his household has come down with a fever and he is very concerned. He is requesting a doctor but could not find one available. He's asking for my assistance. I will go out and see. The man got up but grimaced as he put his wait upon his left foot."

Gabriel noted the discomfort and immediately responded. "Here now, why don't you let me go and make the call? Your housekeeper can show me the way, and I can pick up my medical bag at the lodging house, which is close. You need to stay off that foot. I'll return after I have checked in with the family." Gabriel gently helped the older man back down to his chair.

Dr. Stockton paused for a moment to think over the matter. "Well, I believe that might be a better plan" I'll write a note of introduction. Molly can show you the house. The Thaxtons have been friends for many years. The family has supported the college for some time. I don't want to ignore their request for help in their time of need."

"Thank you, I will send word back as soon as I access what may be the concern. Molly, if you will, show me to the servant who is waiting, and I will get the address."

"Yes, of course, Dr. Hamilton. Follow me."

The Thaxton's home was situated a few blocks down where two-story homes of the federal period lined the street. There was lights lit in the windows in the front rooms of the stately home. The housekeeper ushered Gabriel through the front entrance and to the room on the left, which appeared to be a library. An older gray-haired man stood behind his desk, apparently awaiting the doctor he had requested to attend the ill granddaughter.

"Mr. Thaxton, Dr. Stockton is sick and sends his regrets for not coming in person. This is Dr. Gabriel Hamilton who was at the house of Dr. Stockton's this evening and volunteered to come as the professor's replacement." Mr. Thaxton looked somber, but shook Gabriel's hand.

"Here is a letter of introduction from Dr. Stockton." Gabriel said and offered the letter to Mr. Thaxton.

"I thank you for coming. If you come with Dr. Stockton's recommendations, I am most certainly obliged. I am afraid I am at a loss when it comes to sickness. Please come this way. My granddaughter, Lacey, came home just this morning from caring for some children in the township. It's a long story about her background, but she is also married to my eldest grandson son. She has been in this household since she was ten and I will fill you in later, after you have seen her. Our angel was very tired when she arrived, and she looked flushed. She wanted to rest and when she didn't come down to dinner, I had the housekeeper go in and check on her. She found her very feverish. I immediately wanted to seek medical help. I couldn't reach the family doctor, so I kept trying to find someone I felt was competent. Dr. Stockton has always been a trusted friend of the family, so I eventually called on him this evening."

Gabriel had followed the elderly man up the stairs and to a room on the right which looked like it had been a nursery many years ago. Mr. Thaxton pointed to the door. "This is Lacey's room, doctor. She has been like this for at least the last hour.

Dr. Hamilton could see the flushed face of a young woman; red blotches were beginning to appear on her face and chest as he came closer. For a second, her eyes opened, and she whispered to the housekeeper that she needed a sip of water. The housekeeper provided the porcelain teapot shaped item and gave the patient a few drops of water.

"Thank you." The young women lowered her head back on the pillow.

"Lacey, I am Dr. Hamilton. I came to see if I can help you feel better." Gabriel took his bag, listened to the heart beating inside the woman's chest and felt her forehead. He looked at the complexion and neck and arms. Without giving a hint of what he was thinking, Gabriel put a cool compress over her forehead. She opened her eyes again and this time, they only stared at the image hovering above her.

"Yes, Lacey, I believe you have the measles. But you have a very high fever. Perhaps there is something else going on, too. I believe an additional virus is present. The rash appears very much like a strain of measles."

The patient looked up and tried to speak again, but Gabriel put his finger over his lips. Be quiet now, Mrs. Thaxton. You need your strength. Measles is much more serious when an adult has them than as a child. Have you and your staff had measles, sir?"

The housekeeper nodded her head and said she had them as a child.

Mr. Thaxton nodded his head in agreement. "I will check with other household staff to be sure, sir."

"Yes, I would suggest that all your staff who have not had measles stay at home for the next 10 days. Those on staff members who have had measles already and are not pregnant can stay. I would suggest those who also have family members who are pregnant of have some children should also be asked to stay at home. I recommend no visitors to the home for the next ten days."

"Absolutely sir. Whatever you feel is best, we will do."

"Take the clothes that Mrs. Thaxton brought with her and burn them."

"Yes," the housekeeper said. "She brought so few things, and she didn't even unpack."

"On second thought, do you still have the bag here?" Gabriel asked.

"Yes, I removed nothing when she came. It's right over there," said the housekeeper.

"Okay, don't touch it for now. Let me think for a moment. I don't' want to leave her as her fever may not have peaked and she is still contagious. I do not wish to infect anyone else that I might be in contact with on my journey back home."

"Dr. Hamilton, you can be our guest for as long as you need. We have plenty of rooms and resources to care for your needs and we are indebted to you in this hour of our need. Lolli, can you get master Quintin's room ready for the doctor? I think that will be the most comfortable room. Have you brought your things with you? We can send someone out for them."

"No, I picked up my things when I picked up the medical bag on the way here. I would like to send a message to Dr. Stockton about the circumstances and the change of plans. I need to send a telegram to my family. Is that possible?"

"Yes, I can get someone who has not been in the house to send a message. My sister lives in the home adjoining the back yard. Her staff would be most willing to communicate anything and provide us with supplies as needed. I can telegram from the foundry's office. Please, right the message and we'll send someone down to the office to send it out immediately."

"Thank you, sir. I think Mrs. Thaxton's fever may rise a little more before it breaks. I would like to stay right here for a couple more hours to make sure we don't have to cool her down with an ice bath. Oh, one more question. Do you think there's a chance that Mrs. Thaxton might be pregnant? Measles can have a negative impact on an unborn child."

"No, I don't believe so. Major Thaxton has been serving in the army for the past two years and has not been home. Our dear Lacey was helping with some work at a local church and doing instruction at the orphanage. She is always busy."

"I see," said Dr. Hamilton with no expression. He looked back at his patient. Dr Hamilton thought to himself. *Oh Sam, you have a story, don't you? The pirate of the mountains, the angel in the battlefield and the mysterious courier who slips in and out of military encampments. Who are you, Mrs. Thaxton?*

The housemaid scurried off to complete her chores. Mr. Thaxton eventually agreed to rest in his room. This gave Gabriel time to collect his thoughts. Though he was not sure this was the right thing to do, he walked over to the bag that Mrs.

Hamilton had brought with him and looked inside. Nothing of significance inside would explain what she had been doing the last few months. There was an envelope tucked in the false bottom of the bag. This was the striking match, Gabriel thought. He looked back over at the young women on the bed. She was sleeping but not peacefully at this moment. The patient continued to mumble some things now and then. An envelope with a card was on the bottom of the pouch. He inspected the contents further. Embossed with the hotel's logo in Washington logo where Gabriel had stayed his last night, he thought rather interesting. A pencil sketch of an eagle soaring was hand drawn on the stationery. *Your mission is over, Little Dove. You will not be forgotten.* The handwriting was familiar and so was the sketch. He hurriedly put everything back in the Satchel and went back to bed before anyone came back. She showed more mumbling as time when on with isolated bursts of understandable utterances.

"I can make it. Let me go. I can give him the message. Please let me go," said Sam.

Gabriel heard her plea. Her face was marked with intensity. Her eyes looked into a phantom that she saw her mind. "I can get McPherson through the pass. I know the way through the pass and all they to the gap in the highlands. It's not on a map. My parents knew the way. Please let me show him. Quintin. General Grant. I know the way." She rolled her head from side to side. Gabriel put another wet cloth to her forehead and felt her cheeks. He doused her arms with another press of cool water from the cloth. Her arms showed increased dots since he first arrived. It only seemed like things were getting worse. If the fever didn't break soon, it would not be a good sign. Gabriel sat intently, trying to pick up each word Sam said in her delirium.. Were these the secrets she had been hiding? Perhaps the mysteries were being purged out of her body so that she could live freely again. She must have seen the loss of freedom, life, and dignity in her adventures. Gabe thought how he too must return home with a changed heart than the one he had when he left home. Otherwise, his efforts would be wasted, and he would be sent back to relearn the lesson.

Sam started murmuring again. "Run fast. We must cross the bridge before they blow it up. We must get to the other side. The shortcut is just around the bend. We can make it if I just make it over the bridge." Sam quieted down for a few more minutes.

Gabriel was happy no one had returned yet. He wasn't sure how much her family knew of where she really had been, but Gabriel didn't want to reveal anything.

Suddenly, she stirred again. "John, I won't leave you!" She reached up to touch Gabe's face. "I'm coming back. Hide yourself in the ravine. I will get help. I promise."

Gabe wiped her brow and continued to watch over her. How much did she know, he wondered, or did her delirium brink on fantasies that were never real? She turned and tossed some more. "I promised Grant that I'd make it through. There's the creek. I can hear the water from here. Go and cross the creek. There's a clearing on the other side. My mother's people would come here. The young men played games with other tribes in the clearing. There's a farm with a well at the end of the field." Sam stopped her shifting in the bed and then continued in her delirium." I'm tired. Leave me alone, Hamilton. I can't tell you anything. I didn't steal from the camp. Don't bother me. I just want to sleep."

Gabriel looked at her face. He was there in her thoughts. He tried to soothe her mind with his gentle words. "Sam, you're home now. I know you are tired, but you must fight this fever first. Your grandfather is here. Lolli is here. You're back in your grandfather's home and safe."

Sam opened her eyes for a moment and asked for more water. He gave her a few drops of the tea he had concocted. She took a couple of sips and relaxed her shoulders to put her head back down.

Just then, the housekeeper came back in. "Dr. Hamilton, I've got your room all made up for you. I can sit with Miss. Lacey, while you take a break. I will call you if there's a change."

"Thank you, Mrs. Colton. I will wait another thirty minutes or so with you and then retire for a few hours. I'm not sure I will be much good if I don't get some sleep as I was up during the ride from Washington. I must ask, did Mrs. Thaxton ever go by Sam?"

"Yes, sir." Mrs. Colton gave a little laugh. "When she was younger, she wanted to play with the boys. She was persistent not to be left out. The boys gave her the nickname Sam, and it stuck. I haven't heard her call herself that in years. Now, I've got the ointment just in case she starts to scratch to ease the itch, and I have another pitcher of cool water to help with the fever. Do you think it's too soon to try to give her a little broth if she wakes up?"

"I made a little tincture here with some things from my bag. See if she will take a sip or two when she is awake. I suspect she has a strep infection too that is causing a fever and a sore throat, so I don't think she should have anything solid. Sips of liquids such as broth should be fine when she's alert today. Thank you, Mrs. Colton."

"She is the princess here. Her grandfather would be at a total loss if she left us so young. Lacy's mother looked just like her age. Her Indian name was Morning Dove. Mr. Martin brought her home with him as his wife after being an officer in the Army. His superiors ordered his unit to assist with the removal of the Indians from their lands in Georgia, but he disliked this, so he left the Army and returned to work with his father, starting the pharmacy on the corner. Quintin was the son of Mr. Thaxton's first marriage. Quintin's mother was delicate, but she was young and pampered. Mr. Thaxton's second wife had a bigger heart. She was Lacey's and John's maternal grandmother. Her only son, John Robert Martin, was Lacey and John's father. When the children's parents died on a ship coming back from Savannah, the children lived here permanently with Mr. and Mrs. Thaxton. The children have been a source of the joy in this home. Their grandmother passed away just before the war started in 1861. It's been a difficult time for many families.

We are happy to know the fighting will soon end. This is a household that holds on to faith and treasures each man and women that God created. Now, let me show you Quintin's room. I think you will like it very much. It has a splendid view of the creek that runs alongside the property. He has some of his things on the shelf from the days when he was up north studying. You might know what some things mean. I just keep them dusted." Mrs. Colton continued down the hall. "Here you go," the housekeeper said as she opened the door. "I aired it out for a few minutes and put some fresh linen on the bed. Master Quintin hasn't been home for almost two years now. It will be good for the room to be used again. You may find something that fits your in the chest of drawers."

"Thank you, Ma'am. I am sure I will be quite comfortable."

"Let me get back to Miss Lacey, just in case she has awoken and needs something."

"Yes, I think her condition will change for the better soon. Please call if there is any change." The door closed behind the housekeeper and Gabriel was finally alone. He sat on the bed and unbutton the shirt buttons around his neck. The doctor had wanted to process all the information given, but his mind was too tired to process it all tonight.

The next morning, the housekeeper had been relieved by Mr. Thaxton, who sat quietly reading a passage from Esther in the Bible. I think you must have been a descendant of a princess. You and your mother both.

"Thank you," Lacey said hoarsely. "I am tired, grandfather, but I will be fine. You need to stay away so that you don't get what I have. It would not go well with you to get sick because of me."

"That may be true, but I want to be sure you are out of the woods. Dr. Hamilton has agreed to stay with us for a week to look in on you and to quarantine himself so that he does not transmit anything to others he may pass on his way back home. We were fortunate to have him visiting when he was. He was visiting Dr. Stockton at the time your fever rose yesterday, and you needed medical attention. Dr. Hamilton was kind enough to respond to our request. He will check on you a bit later. He had a very long day yesterday."

"My head is not completely clear, but you mentioned Dr. Hamilton was here," Lacey croaked out with her voice taxed with laryngitis.

"Yes, he will be with us for a few days, just as a precaution, of course. We would hate to spread the measles around town. "

Lacey showed agony on her face.

"Don't worry dear, he was a proper gentleman the whole time. Lolli made sure there was no impropriety. She helped you with all bathing and dressing." Mr. Thaxton winked at Lacey and tapped her hand.

"I think I would like to rest some more this morning. I would like to get out of bed by noon, even if it is to sit by the window. I do not wish to leave this room until these red dots are gone."

"Yes, that is all fine with us. We want you in tiptop shape. Once you're feeling better, we'll take a ride in the carriage and take you to the milliners and the dressmakers and you can get anything you heart desires."

"Thank you, grandfather. I promise to get better. I didn't mean to come home and be sick."

"Of course, not my dear one, but we will get you back healthy in no time. You are a bit on the thin side if you ask me, so I'll be sure to have Lolli make your favorites as soon as Dr. Hamilton says it is okay."

Lacey croaked a sound out of irritation.

By day seven, the patient looked clear of spots and Lacey's energy level was back to taking meals in the breakfast room in the morning. Her aunt had stopped by the dressmaker to pick up a couple of new day dresses that would suit her niece's coloring and sent them over with the day's supply of fresh bread from the bakery and a half slab of ham and some jars of green beans and jams from her pantry.

Gabriel's time was at its end. It was now time to thank the Thaxtons for their hospitality and allow Lacey to continue her natural course of recovery. She was out of the stages of danger and being contagious. She might be weak for a few more weeks, but her condition prior to her arrival may have led to the seriousness of her symptoms.

Gabriel had spent very little time with his patient alone, and perhaps that is how it should be. He knew now that a brotherhood of individuals who had a mission larger than themselves had protected her. Warriors, healers, engineers, and administrators had their purposes. The doves that flew in secret coves and ravines by night had their missions, too. Gabriel would have to be at peace for now on what he had learned, if anything, more than just a few more dots to add to the mystery.

Lacey walked with her grandfather, with her arm linked with his, to the front entryway as Gabriel picked up his medicine bag. The groomsman loaded a small truck in the back of the carriage that Gabriel's father had sent as soon as he got word of when his son would be leaving the city.

Dr. Hamilton found Lacey in the garden this morning upon arriving downstairs. You are a vision of health this morning, Mrs. Thaxton.

"Thank you, Dr. Hamilton. I believe lavender is my color rather than red polka dots. My grandfather and I hope you will return in the future when you come to Philadelphia. I would like to race you on horseback between lampposts in the park or sail on a schooner down the river."

"Yes, I would like that very much, too. I plan to come to Philadelphia again soon. I would enjoy meeting your brother and your husband again when he returns. I met Quintin at the hotel the night before I left for Philadelphia."

Lacey presented a polite smile. "Did you? I'm very glad. Quintin is a protective man with his time. He was very busy in Washington that week from what he told us in his telegram. If he made time to see you in Washington, then he wanted to make your acquaintance. He does not do that for everyone."

Dr. Hamilton bowed his head to hide the blush he was starting to feel on his cheeks. "I believe it was just by chance that we met. I thank you for the compliment, though." Gabe knew he was being charmed into liking this woman. This time he somehow allowed the arrow to hit his heart without a deflecting comment. He knew it was time to run fast before she put the netting over his head, and he'd be caught forever. She was a married woman. He completely understood the boundaries. He would be riding away in the sunset, just like a pirate or a musketeer. "Did you leave this in my things when I was sick? Lacey asked. Her violet eyes were narrowing as she held a small box in her hand.

"No. I swear I didn't." Gabe looked into her face dumbfounded.

"Where did this come from then?" Lacey asked rather perturbed.

"I'm not sure, but I can assure you it was not me." Gabe responded

"What did I talk about when I was sick?"

"Only rambling. No one was in the room while I was in the room. I told no one anything except what your condition was." Dr. Hamilton responded. Gabe caught movement in the kitchen and thought this might be his cue to see who else might be up. He could pour a cup of coffee in the breakfast room to help change the subject. He told Lacey he would be right back. Just as Gabe got up he saw what the commotion was all about.

Lacey instead looked down at the box with concern. "Who's been here?" she whispered. Concern showed on her face.

"Something has got my wife in a dither today. Did I forget to send enough to pay the account at the Milner's on the corner?"

Lacey swung herself around. "Quintin!" squealed Lacey. She jumped up than ran to his arms. In an instant, her mood changed, "Quintin, it's really you?"

"Undeniably, in the flesh." Major Thaxton turned to great the other man in the garden. "Dr. Hamilton, the good doctor. My father wired me to let me know that Lacey was sick and that you, by my surprise, were here to help her through the blight of measles." Quintin looked back at his wife. "I had them as a child, sweety. It' will not scare me away. I tried to get here sooner, but I got delayed from leaving Washington."

"This box, did it come from you?" Lacey asked with excitement.

"Yes, I must confess. I slipped in late last night and didn't want to wake you. I made sure you come across this morning when you got dressed."

"You scared me with that. I thought there may have been an intruder," She smiled up and looked at her husband with her violet eyes that glistened with her tears. I would have had to have grandfather guard our home with extra security. They may have even kept the likes of you coming in when you haven't washed," said Lucy between her giggles.. "I am so happy it was you! However, sneaking in my personal undergarments, sir, is against the rules of a gentleman in the household. The military has not served you well, considering etiquette in a lady's boudoir."

"That may be true mam, but it sure was fun!"

"Shush, you are going to embarrass me," said Lacey with humor.

"Yes, and as usual, you started it, and someone will put me in the puppy house for mischief, just like when we were kids." Well, now that you know, we can open it later."

Major Thaxton turned to the side and had put out his hand to shake Dr. Hamilton's hand. "Dr. Hamilton, I'm so happy to see again. You've been helping my wife recover, I understand, and I am extremely grateful for that. Is there anything I need to know to keep continuing her progress?"

"No, she is doing well and should not have any complications. I was actually leaving the city today to return to my family's home for a few days. My solicitor has been looking at some potential rentals intown. I have not completely decided on my next move."

Quintin smiled back. "That is completely understandable and I am excited for you. I am ready to start a new just like you, although my new, maybe just to return to my family. I am happy here.

Gabriel saw what he was waiting for. "I see Pepper coming now." The groomsman's son had brought him up from the stables just down the street. Pepper's trot grew faster as it came closer to the gathering. Dr. Hamilton stood and spoke to slow the horse down, and Pepper obeyed while Gabriel rubbed his neck. However, even that had not completely quieted his old companion, and he nudged his master's arm .

Lacey picked up the sign and walked down the steps to the horse. Perhaps he smelled the sweet treats in her hand. Dr. Hamilton. please allow me to offer our old friend a treat. Pepper nibbled the sugar cubes from the hand of the young lady. She whispered in his ear. "Yes, Pepper, you like your treats, don't you? But it's time to go to your new home, my old friend," Lacey looked at Gabriel. "I think your friend is ready now."

"Mrs. Thaxton, you have a way with horses." Dr. Hamilton responded at the sight of the horse nibbling out of the young women's hand. He then turned to the young boy and said. "I'll ride her until we reach the outskirts of town. Gilly, take up with your father. I think Pepper is just a little nervous this morning."

The young women stepped away. After giving the horse the last cubes of sugar in her pocket. "There now, you shall have a safe and speedy journey home." Lacey walked to the top of the steps to the home as the doctor motioned for the horse to move on.

Gabriel took the rains and felt the pull back to stable that was past the Thaxton's home. Gabriel stopped to ponder. What's the matter, Pepper? It's time for us to go home, where you'll have a full pasture to roam. After a couple more nudges by Gabriel's thighs, the horse moved toward where it was being led.

Her grandfather patted her hand and led her back inside as their guest started out. "I think I see new life on the trees already.

It means so much to see signs of new beginnings and through the winter gloom. Let's go back inside, dear, before you get sick again. There will be time to be outdoors in the sunshine, you'll see."

Chapter 9

Going Home

Gabriel returned to Salt Lick Farm, a place carved out of two streams that came together and flowed into the larger river that eventually flowed to the Atlantic. Summer crops lined the pike with small villages between them until he finally met the hamlet where his father lived. He could see the tall stalks of corn that his father always planted in the backfield. Cucumbers, pepper, lettuce, and cabbage were in a garden closer to the house. The signs of potatoes, carrots, onions and beets dotted the garden next to the smokehouse. In the fall, the kitchen would be full of activity with canning and preserving for the winter. It was the harvest ritual. It was good to see the field stone house again, just as he left it three years ago. The war destroyed much of the farmland in the southern states. He couldn't erase the memories, but he could appreciate seeing the simple blessings that he now appreciated more than ever. Gabriel had to be honest that in the past, he never thought of how the jarred green beans and potatoes came to be on the table and ready to eat a warm meal in the cold winter months. He never would ignore the importance of the cycles of life after experiencing life in the military camps.

As the party arrived at their destination, the house came alive. Gabriel had made it home. His family welcomed him back with tears and hugs. The soldier came back into the arms of his family. Later that evening, Gabriel and his father had some quiet time alone on the back porch.

"Gabriel, I don't think you have listened to a word I said."

"I'm sorry, father. My mind was on some other things. You were saying something about Mr. Arnold."

"Yes, I was talking about Ted Arnold and how you should make an appointment to see him this week. I think he will give you some good news. He asks about you every time I see him."

"Yes, I promise. He wrote me letters here and there, but he always kept some details vague. I don't think he wanted anyone to receive confidential information. He always told me where I could contact him should I need the actual figures for some of my investments."

"He's a good man. I've never questioned his judgment on things."

"He asked me if I wanted to be a partner in a few ventures in the western part of the state before I left the military. It sounded like a promising venture. I do need to give him an answer. I just have had other things on my minds since I left Washington."

"That's understandable." Gabriel's father paused before making his next inquiry. "How is your patient in the city? You did say something that you knew them from when you were in the military. Was your patient a former soldier?"

"It was just a case of measles."

"Oh, so it was a child you were caring for?" His father raised his eyebrows in interest.

"I was caring for Mrs. Thaxton. She is married to Major Quintin Thaxton. Have you heard of him or the family?"

"So it was a female you were caring for that kept you away from us?"

"Father, that is not what I meant as the reason for my delay in coming home. I have told you enough. It was a complete accident, really. I was available while a friend of mine was ill and unable to help. Once I arrived, I realized who she was. I knew her husband from the military."

"Measles you say?"

"Have you been listening to me? I went to see her for my friend who was sick. That's it. I'm not telling you one more thing. I think I will take my coffee back up to my room."

"Oh Gabriel, don't do that. I've missed our conversations. I won't say another word on the subject. Are you contemplating setting up a practice in Philadelphia?"

"I don't know. I don't like the risks of serving in a city with mass epidemics like yellow fever that plaque the port towns.

However, I will explore all options and take on what seems like the right fit. I have an offer to go back to Washington, but I would like some distance from there for a while."

"That's understandable. War is an awful thing to experience. Of course, the decision is yours. I am happy to have you at home with me. You look so grown up now. It's hard to believe how much three years have changed your countenance. I am proud of you, son, for all that you did to help those soldiers."

"Whatever I did to serve those men didn't come from me, father. I can't control if this man will live or that will die. I can only do what I know to be true for the moment and leave the rest in the power that heals that is above any human source."

"Ah Gabriel, have you come to believe in God?" his father asked.

"I believe in something that is larger than me being involved in the fate of man. On the battlefield I saw the fiery eyes in a soldier's eyes that defied the odds against him. I watched the mercy pour from a man's soul as he provided sips of water while holding a dying enemy in his arms. Then there was the nurturing love of a young wife who washed and cleansed the facial wound and arm of a blood-soaked officer and brought him back to health only to see another day. Yes, father, those moments have touched me in profoundly. I have had my own personal touch of something I can't explain yet. That unknown met me on a mountain in a gap in Georgia. A face tinged with dirt and clothes covered with straw has followed me for the last three years. Why that something chose to follow me I can't say, but I know it was real, and it found where I was at that time in my soul. I may have started seeking something to fill my life in a different way, but now I know I've changed my path and I'm seeking that which found me and led me from there to home.

"Oh Gabriel, your mother heard those words and is weeping with joy somewhere out there. We never wanted to raise in a manner that would push you away from finding God. Each man has to do that on his own terms."

"Thank you, father. I know you and mother love me and that's all that matters. It's good to be home!" Gabriel's eyes teared up, and he gave his father a hug. "It's time for me to finish this coffee. We'll talk more in the morning when I get back after checking on some things."

Several hours away in a city still buzzing with the sounds of moving wagons and trains whistling. The elder Thaxton had returned upstairs for the night. His son was left alone with his wife in the front parlor.

****

"You didn't eat much this evening. Are you filling alright?" Lacey asked her husband.

"Absolutely, I just need to be home more often and eat food more food that I grew up with eating."

"I thought you ate well as an officer?"

"Of course. Our provisions were plentiful and the best the Army had. I was just complaining when I shouldn't have been. Let's change the subject. I don't want to talk about that now.

I think the diamond looks extremely pretty on you?" Quintin brushed a tendril from her shoulder.

"Yes, it is. It is beautiful. She looked out the window at the stars and found the star that she felt looked the most like the brilliance. "When did you find it?"

"It was part of a collection of stones from my mother. I've been keeping them safe. I had had the jeweler downtown create the necklace. I was to give it to you on our anniversary, but I couldn't get back here."

"How do you think your mother acquired them? Adventures, maybe?" Lacy smiled back with mischief in her eyes.

"Could have been? My great grandfather was reportedly a man of the sea. We were never to reveal his history." Quintin replied. "My father inherited quite a chest of things when his father passed on. I haven't seen everything, but I know many things were obtained in the late 1700s from the things I have seen so far."

"Interesting," Lacey said with a grin. "Does that mean my husband maybe directly descended by a pirate or great grandfather leader like Rollo?"

"I see where this is leading. I'm hoping you'll be content with being Mrs. Thaxton and not the wild child you've been as of late."

"I don't know. I think it's in my blood." Lacey said. She reached for her husband's hand and turned off the parlor light.

Chapter 10

Dove on the Loose

Gabriel's yearning stood in his way of staying with his parents for long. He had corresponded with a physician in New York who was working on developing techniques to rebuild facial injuries through surgical techniques. He had learned about the physician's work while at the field hospital and he was so intrigued by what could be done to help the disfigurement for the soldiers who survived these horrendous wounds. Some wounds were so ghastly they he could not talk about them to his family, but they still haunted him. He wanted to learn more about what could be done. He could bring those skills back to the hospital in Philadelphia. If Lacey waited, perhaps he would ask her for a commitment. He suspected his heart had already made a choice, but he was not ready to listen just yet. Gabriel had never showed any commitment to any female before. He wasn't sure he was capable of it. He decided on New York as his next temporary home. Yes, that is what he would do. Gabriel sent a telegram to his friend in New York and accepted the position offered.

Months had gone by since he left the military hospitals. Gabriel stayed in touch with many of his old friends and developed inspiration by many of his new acquaintances. This led to a variety of stimulating evenings and holidays. Gabriel was missing his friends in the city. Gabriel made plans to visits the Thaxton's the first weekend in November. Yes, there was a chill in the air, but he remembered the warmth of a heart that was living with compassion and energy.

Surprise was what Gabriel felt on the day he arrived on two accounts. The first surprise came when he made his way to visit with the Thaxton's, the housekeeper ushered him into the library. Quintin Thaxton stood up to meet his guest. "Well, Gabriel, how nice to have you come and visit. My father will be down shortly. He just went up to put on a change of clothes. I knew you wouldn't mind his overall's, but even at his age he doesn't like to meet guest with less than his Sunday best."

Gabriel smiled and shot the younger Thaxton's hand. He remembered another Thaxton in overalls and almost let out a laugh. "So, are your home now for good or are you returning to the military?"

"No, I am not going back to the military. I may be going back to Washington, though."

"Really,? Doing what?"

"Sam Grant and I have been friends for a long time. I am also intrigued by some other offers related to steel and railroads. Right now, I am working with my father, helping him keep the foundry up and going. I will see what the future holds."

"Is your wife at home?" Gabriel asked.

"No, she is in New York, as I'm speaking. My aunt swooped her away. I don't think she really wanted to go, but another friend's family and my grandfather arranged it. My grandfather insisted she go to brighten her spirits.

"Has she been unwell?" Gabriel expressed concern in his voice.

"Not as far as I know. We've received a letter yesterday saying the weather was very disagreeable, but the people she was staying with were friendly. There is some connection with a family in Savannah and a young lady named Annabella who she went to finishing school when she was younger. Reportedly,the family has their own shipping line. It sounds like she is doing the things the young ladies would like. Balls, teas, and the new dresses are what she talks about, mostly. Occasionally, she will throw in something of genuine interest. Supposedly, she has met a prime minister at a dinner party."

Gabriel's heart fell just a little as Quintin talked about his wife. His heart stirred yet; these influential men of the world would never Gabriel's true jealousy. They had a something in their world that would never truly be his. Gabriel held back a laugh. *Wonder what finishing school* taught young *ladies to run at full speed through the night through forests and* over hedges.

He let his thoughts ponder the image of ladies riding full saddle,not the side saddle of debutantes. She learned somewhere. How else would she know how to jump over hedges and leap over gullies? Her use of languages to code messages could be very useful and highly desired by a prominent government official or military general. She learned *to ride* bareback *from her mother's* people, *he supposed. She was a dove,set loose to be free and come and go as she pleased. Who could keep her bound?* Footsteps were coming from the hall, and then a familiar voice floated through the room.

The elder Thaxton had returned donning a day suite. "Gabriel, we are so happy to see you again! You will stay for lunch, won't you?"

"Of course," Gabriel responded and shook the man's hand.

"You've heard already that our lovely Lacey is away presently.She recovered fine in body, but I think the trip will do her spirit some *good.She needed something to put adventure back in her cap again, right Quintin."*

Gabriel almost coughed on the scotch he was tasting, but held the cough back as the rim around his eyes burned.

"Yes." Quintin said with no expression on his face.

"I thought I would visit before I continue my trip to New York myself. I have an offer that I am investigating there at least short term. I would like more experience in doing facial reconstruction surgery. After sometime with Dr. Ketchum, I might explore some additional options."

"Wherever the wind takes you, we wish you well. Things are changing so rapidly. I can't believe I am seeing what I am seeing in my lifetime. Trains getting us in days not weeks. Then there is all the new factories and industries rising. Their making steel building and bridges now. I can see a day when they will figure out how to make us fly in the air, but I won't be around to see that I'm afraid," the elder Thaxton said.

Quintin led his grandfather in the diningroom while the gentleman continued to talk. "Grandfather, you have been very busy with providing iron products for a while. Where do you think the next industry will be?"

"That's my grandson, Gabriel, always wanting to think about the future. You know Quintin, it may be time for us to change our interests in the foundry. Times are changing. Energy is going to be an area that everyone is going to need with all the new machinery that is being invented. Development of different energy sources for large scale public use, I think, will be on people's minds."

"There is some talk of drilling for oil as a source. The country will need trained engineers."

"That is true. That's why I wanted Quintin to have the experience of being an engineer now that he is young. After some experience, he can explore how he would like to use his training. Some people naturally fall into their calling, but others have to follow the adventure of finding out their purpose."

Gabriel looked up at the elder Thaxton and tried to read a deeper message that was in the man's thoughts. Perhaps there was no deeper message, but it lit something inside Gabriel's heart. He yearned to ask more questions, but held his lips closed for now.

Quintin chimed in to the conversation. "Mining has been around since Soloman. We think we are doing something new, but in fact the concepts have been around since the earliest times. The secrets of how the ancients could accomplish what they did were a passion for me when I studied engineering. The ability to work always has a source of energy from somewhere. Finding a source of energy to sustain life is key."

"That's one idea. Hydro energy is being used to create steam .We've seen that being used for boats and trains. There are certainly some opportunities to explore and question if steam is a long-term viable energy source and can it serve other purposes." Quintin added.

Gabriel listened to the conversation at lunch. There was a lot being shared between the gifted minds. Gabriel understood why Quintin'sexpertise was so important to the military. Lacey's brother had a keen understanding of how machinery worked. "You know, I saw a need for the need for sterilization of medical tools. I believe there is someone working on an antiseptic solution, but what about a machine that could also clean items of things we can't see?"

"Gabriel, that's a really great idea. Sanitation is paramount. I like where your mind is going. We haven't been involved in medicine. Quintin, Ithink we might want to explore some of those ideas more actively. There may bean opportunity for us to develop something that is really needed," the older man said at the table. The elder Thaxton took another bite of the soup that satin front of him.

Quintin added, "I like it too. We don't want to spread ourselves too thin, but I think we need to change the business to make ourselves relevant now that the war is ending. Machinery is changing our world?"

"I'm getting old, Gabriel; we need some young minds out there creating new ways of doing things."

Gabriel accepted the praise with a smile towards Quintin's grandfather. "Is this the way it always is at lunch at your home?"

"This stuff. Oh yes! My grandparents always allowed us to sit at the grownup's table growing up. We listened to conversations during meals when visitors came. My grandparents freely discussed topics around the table. It was quite different at many of my friends' homes, you know, needing to sit at the kid's table for parties in another room. My friends from school always said their families were boring after spending time here." Quintin said.

"My wife and I always enjoyed the extra company. Once I reached my midlife years and I could work for myself, I tried to come home for lunch when I could, and I made it my rule to be home for dinner unless there was an emergency. There were times I had to be away, but few. You and Lacey behaved like angels and never gave us a bit of trouble."

"Well, I don't know about that." Quintin looked up at Gabriel and winked. "It's what you don't know, grandfather that has kept you from not growing bald all these years."

"That may be true. You would think after growing up in the same household for part of their lives, the two would have found out enough about each other not to spend a lifetime together." The elder responded with warmth in his eyes. All the children growing up under this roof were blessings. He chuckled for a second before casting his eyes on his guest. "Gabriel, how can we help you in New York on your visit? Do you have friends that you are staying with while you are in town?"

"Actually, I am planning on staying with an aunt and uncle who live a few blocks away from my one of my appointments later in the week. I will have easy access to transportation to get around once I get that far, I hope."

"That is superb! We have connections up that way." The elder gentleman added nothing more. His silence revealed the wisdom of a mind at work. "The river valley is beautiful. I'm sure the residents in those villages would love having your medical services. My wife and I spent several summers while Quintin was at school there."

"Yes, I've had thought of that. My father said he was thinking of moving on himself. He knows his time of working the farm is ending. He was always a businessperson, and I think he is waiting for me to decide on my next move before he makes his. Of course, wherever I go, I would want him to be near. There was never an idea that I would abandon him now that he is getting on in years."

The conversation flowed for some time after lunch. However, it was nearing three o'clock and Gabriel knew he would need to leave to catch his train on time to get to the city. He was sincerely sad to leave. The smell of the freshly made coffee after dinner still filled his nostrils. He felt the genuine welcome deep in his heart. He also stored the memory of the portrait that hung in the hall. It would remain with Gabriel during the ride to New York. He was happy that Quintin had time to take him to the train station. There was a lot that Quintin and he had in common. Quintin himself was taking a train back to Washington for an assignment the next day, Though the fighting had mostly stopped, there still were military operations in place that required Quintin'sexpertise.

Mr. Thaxton, the elder, had an idea of his own. In the morning, he would send a telegraph to his acquaintance in New York. An introduction to some strategic people would support his plan.

Gabriel had found his way to a hotel in the city when his train arrived the first night in the city near the new park. He had personal business at his solicitor's office to attend regarding investments his father had set up for him while he was gone. Gabriel also had an appointment with the surgeon who he had been in correspondence with over the last few months. He was lucky to be within walking distance of both. Dr. Brooks was kind enough to invite him to dinner at his home that evening. A small soiree planned by his wife as a welcoming gesture was on the agenda. The evening was interesting was and very enjoyable with a robust conversation afterwards in the library.

"Dr. Hamilton, have you confirmed what your plan is now that you have left the military?"

"No yet. I am exploring some ideas that I was considering while I was still in Washington. I want to come home and visit my family before I made any commitments. I am traveling further north the next couple of days and visiting with my uncle and his wife. I have no interest in the textile mills that my uncle has invested in. The world of medicine will make great strides because of the war. The opportunity for changing the way we heal people's wounds and diseases will change because of the horror we have seen over the past 4 years. If there is a benefit from what we have learned from this war, it is that we can do things better."

"I would agree with that," stated Dr. Brooks.

"I have been reading about some work regarding antiseptics and antibiotics.It seems very promising," said another man in the group.

"With the election coming soon and your experience with the Washington set, I think you would in move toward providing services meaningfully to our veterans."

"I am not opposed to sharing what I know. However, my influence needs to be considered with other ideas as well for the most prudent plan of action. I'm not one to say only my ideas are the most important."

"Well said, I know your work has led you here to our state, and we would be very happy to have you here in the city ." another man spoke upstanding by the fireplace.

"Yes, Dr. Hamilton, we would very much like to have you here, "Dr Brooks warmly smiled. "However, I want you to be sure that his is what you want. You say you're going to the academy after this. The countryside is beautiful, and the river lies hold to many homes of wealthy families. Then there's the military influence that you have. Perhaps your interest is in teaching the sciences?"

"I am exploring my opportunities. I think my taste for certain goals has changed since I served in the military. It's not that I am eager to recall some of the horrific signs and sounds of war. I think my heart has more compassion now than it did going into the profession, and I would like to build on that motivation. Something happened to me when I was in the field hospital."

"You would have to be a man of iron, not to let it affect you,"said Dr. Brooks.

"Well, I say I'm glad it's nearly over and we can move on towards normal again."

Gabriel nodded affirmatively. In his heart, there was a tender spot for all those who had experienced the impact of the war directly. The faces of men he saw on the marches as they passed by the medical tents he would never forget. Souls marching onward. They didn't need to share words as they passed by their faces so much. His heart hadn't forgotten them. Gabriel just wanted to find his way to do more. He suddenly felt the need for fresh air and spoke up. "I hate to leave first, but I need to return to my hotel. It has been a pleasure to meet you."

"Dr. Hamilton, my groomsman and carriage are waiting outside,please let me give you a ride back," said one man. "It's time for me to get back as well."

"Thank you, Mr. Ingram. I will take you up on that kind offer. "The ridge to the hotel near the train station was several blocks away. The two men in the carriage continued to converse on the way to the hotel. "I will see that you receive an invitation to dinner at the Clarks tomorrow evening. There will be some people there that you would enjoy meeting. It will be a small gathering, I'm sure, but an interesting group and influential men and women in their own way."

Gabriel looked over at the man sitting across from him. "Why is that?"

Mr. Ingrams responded, "Well, the Clarks are relatives of the Van Dorns. The Van Dorns gained their family holdings in shipping when the grandfather passed away. They invested a good deal of their wealth in the railroad now, along with some other business interests. I believe you said you knew the Thaxtons? The grandson has invested a lot of time in understanding the mechanics and operations of it all. He's one of the best engineers in the county. Have you met this young man?"

"Interesting that you should ask. Yes, I met him during the war briefly and met up with him prior to coming here. He had taken some leave to check on things at home." Gabriel shared no further information about his previous relationship with the Thaxton's wife.

"I believe his wife, Lacey, and her aunt are visiting the Clarks as we speak. You could meet up again during your stay. The grandfather doesn't travel as much now that he is older. He has as interesting life story. He came to America as an indentured servant landing in Savannah, along with two other boys his age. They made their fortunes in different ways. Mr. Thaxton and one boy eventually settled in the city where the Thaxtons are now, and they married sisters. The sisters have family ties with the Clarks. The boy remained in Georgia and raised his family as he build his fortune. That was the heart-breaking thing about this war. Men fought each other who is some cases where fighting those they had deep respect and affection that went deep. It's painful to see the land covered in blood."

"Yes, the loss was great. The scars are real. More so is the terrifying thought if we didn't get the lesson right this time, we'll see it again in the future. Well, I see the hotel right up the street. Thank you for the ride back. I shall be leaving by train in the morning."

Gabriel returned to his room. This gave him a chance to write a quick note to his father. He wrote some things down on a personal journal he kept since the time he left for the military. It helped him organize his ideas and keep them as a reference. Most of the information was trivial, but it allowed him to keep a record of thoughts and ideas he was gaining. The next morning started late for Gabriel. He had gone to the breakfast room at the hotel for some coffee and something light to hold him until his next stop. He found a perfect spot by the windows. The server had provided a complimentary newspaper along with the coffee and a warm English muffin. Gabriel accepted the morning hospitality while his attention focused on details of the headlines from the press. He read "Terror on the Tracks in Georgia." A train loaded with Army supplies had been attacked outside Chattanooga. Apparently, there had been some train robbers who planned an attack on a southbound track loaded with supplies. The last of the two cars and the caboose were flipped on their sides, causing injuries. Apparently, there was also a fire after the impact, resulting in multiple deaths at the front of the train. *Most* likely, *the boiler caught fire and* exploded, Gabriel thought.Gabriel went on to note that the train was carrying supplies for the war-scarred Georgia under the protection of the Army as a humanitarian effort. The war was over for the small communities along the road in the northern part of the state where the likes of Generals Thomas, McPherson, Hooker commanded by general Sherman had clashed with their counter parts Hood, Cheatam, Gordan and Claiborne. Images of these generals' human forms would fade as the years moved on, but Gabriel experienced their presence firsthand. The smell of the tobacco, the twinkle in the eye when the Scotsman laughed. Then there was the Irish brogue that drifted down the stream alerting Gabriel that danger was near when he stopped bathing in a pool of water under a fall and moved toward safety hiding in the thick ancient rhododendron and mountain laurel near the headwaters in the gap. He did not want to romanticize these memories too much. Gabriel turned the page tosome brighter news and soon gave up, folding the paper and placing it on the chairnext patron. He sipped his coffee and made some notes in his notebook he alwayscarried. A voice boomed from his left and he heard a familiar voice.

"Doc Hamilton, is that you?" Gabriel turned to the sound andstood up to greet an old friend.

"Marcus!" *That rumble of a thunder couldn't be from any-oneelse* Gabriel thought.

"Puts a song in your ears doesn't it my boy!" Marcus gave hisold friend a big smile and a bear hug. "So what has you in the big city, doctor?Taking some time off from for a little pleasure are you?"

"No! Less interesting than that. I was actually here lookingfor my next job. Does that shock you? Now that I am out of the military I canlook at some other options," said Gabriel. He had to admit it felt good to seehis old colleague.

Marcus's voice quieted down. "Well, we can fix that very quickly if you're looking around here. I have friends you see. Lots of friends, and most of them owe me a favor or two."

"Thanks, I know you mean that. Come sit down." Gabriel motioned to the chair across the table from him. His friend sat down and motioned the server to come this way. "I'm too proud to ask for a good word here or there,but I'm not sure this is my calling yet. I stopped in to talk to one of my old instructors at the college when I arrived from Washington a few weeks back.

I then had some personal things to attend. This trip I've been talking with a new group of acquaintances about some other options. Then some people asked me to come to New York to talk with some people at the academy. I was on my way there this morning."

"Well, you are following in the tracks of our former leaders, I see. That's beautiful land around the Hudson River and lots of wealthy people live there, if that's what you are looking for."

"So I've been told already." Gabe responded.

"Money seems to fertilize money, I guess. Seems like you passed through those pastures when you first arrived in Washington as a fresh pup out of college." Marcus looked intently at his friend.

"That is true. I guess that's my reservations with all those that I have spoken with since I have been home. The offers have been interesting and tempting. I'm thinking I have changed some over the last couple of years and maybe in a good way. I don't think I'm looking for exactly that now."

"Well, do you have an idea of what you want?"

"No, not yet. I don't know it's out there."

"Fair enough. You can always keep working on something until your next venture is ready for you. I personally like to keep my hand on a lot of different things. Speaking of whether you stay in town long enough, I will get you a jar of my tomatoes . I use them in everything.

"People used to think that tomatoes were poisonous?" Gabriel smiled.

"You know that's just medieval thinking. They are great for vitamins and working on some sauces them that are quite tasty." Marcus said.

Gabe smiled. "So, are you thinking of putting a label on these jars and giving a name to market the concoction?"

"Well, my idea hasn't gotten that perfected yet, but someday you will see. It's going to be in everyone's pantry across the state."

"Let's think big demand. Let's make it the whole United States," Gabe said with laughter.

"I like that! It could be perfected with the finest brew of tomatoes and exotic spices."

Gabriel laughed out loud. It felt good to be conversing with his old friend on jovial topics just like they did as they rested after their rounds at the field hospital. It was these private times where silly ideas were born. Some of this camp talk turned into brilliant solutions for problems they were plaguing the men.

"Are you home for good now, Marcus, or will you go back?"

"I'm a lifer, I guess. Yes, I'm going back. Now that the war is winding down, the commanders have has been good about giving men some leave. This was my first chance to get outside of a hospital in a while. My wife and I define living near lots of people as our part of our ideal home. We like the civilized comforts of museums and colleges. A good tailor in the area is necessary. My wife likes her charity work and being close to other ladies who like fashion and English-style teas. Lord, help me if I get sent out west."

The men continued their conversation for several more minutes until an arrival of a sound bound train steered away
Gabriel's attention. It was must have been the first train out of
the station from wherever it came from. Once the train came to
a stop, a few patrons came off the train and others lined up to
take their seats. Still others continued to stay on board. Gabriel
glanced up at the train and the passengers remaining on board.
Something took his attention to the last car."Marcus, I think I
need to check on something. Let's keep in touch." He swiftly
pulled out a bill and left in on the table. Gabriel picked up his
personal bag that he had stored under the table and dashed off.

Marcus watched his friend dash off and wondered what had
taken his attention. His eyes dashed a glance at the newspaper
on the other and looked up. His face turned a slight shade of
gray and looked again at the train. There were two women
sitting near the back of one car. The younger of the two was
near the window. Both wore black, from what Gabriel could see.
The ladies started to rise and followed out toward the back. The
younger female wore her hair put up under a hat with a short veil
over her eyes. Gabriel recognized the face in spite of the dreary
black garments with only a bit of white lace around the collar. It
was Lacey Thaxton on board. He darted up from his bench and
walked quickly to the car. Gabriel had just reached the entrance
of the train. The conductor attempted to hold Gabriel back.

"Gabriel, let the man do his job." He heard the rough growl
of a voice behind him. Marcus, who anticipated the scenario,
had crossed the distance in double time. The first of the two

ladies emerged from within the car. Her somber look was noted. "Mrs. Jennings," said Marcus as he placed himself in view. "May I be of some assistance to you ladies?"

"Thank you, sir. We are looking for my houseman, Mr. Higgs. He was to meet up with a carriage. Perhaps we arrived just a bit early as we made good time from where we were staying. Perhaps I could bother you by helping us to collect our bags. My niece is with me."

"Yes, mam. I will assist in any way I can."

"Did someone from the Army send you here, perchance?"

"No mam. "I stopped to chat with my friend, Dr. Hamilton. I ran into him at the hotel across the street. He recognized you and wanted to come and assist. I followed him in his quest to assist you."

"Thank you. Both of you for being such the gentleman."

Lacey emerged from the train. Gabriel said nothing but took her hand. She smiled briefly and walked towards a clearing away from the people who had gathered around the train. "Yes, thank you both for assisting us. I am afraid I'm not quiet myself. The doctor that was sent gave me a sedative in my tea and I don't' think it has worn off. I' m not such a great chaperone for my aunt right now."

"You are doing fine dear and look who God has sent to help us here at the train station. We' will be fine."

"Gabriel, I'm going to find the bags. Mrs. Jennings, please, if you may point out those that are yours."

"Lacey, what has happened?" Gabriel gently asked.

She began to sob."Gabriel," The moment passed, and Lacey heard another voice.

"Mrs. Thaxton, we are sorry about your loss," said a man in a black suit who stood a few yards away."

Lacey stiffened again and put on her stoic face. "Thank you, Mr. Godfrey. Has John arrived yet?" Lacey took a few stops closer to shake the man's hand. She was not able to speak of her brother in the past yet.

"No, mam." The man in black responded. We were told the train will be arriving on Friday. Your husband sent me a telegram with your wishes. He will travel on the same train. I have a carriage waiting for you and your aunt."

"Thank you; I wish to be taken to my grandfather's home for now. Can you take us there?"

"Yes, Mrs. Thaxton. That's why I am here. I am available for you."

"Thank you, Mr. Godfrey. I think we are ready, thanks to our two chivalrous officers. My aunt can help let you know which pieces to load on the carriage. Let me say a few words of gratitude to Major Hamilton and Major McDaniel."

Lacey reached the spot where both of the officers gathered to say a brief goodbye. "I want you to know how much I appreciate your assistance this morning. My brother, John Martin, died in the train explosion south of Chattanooga yesterday. He was helping with the distribution of medicines along with some other needed supplies that were requested for emergency purposes as the supplies had dwindled to nothing prior to the surrender. The transportation routes have been mostly rebuilt in the last few months. Both of you, being physicians and working in the field hospitals in the war, can understand how important it was to get supplies to sites that were needed. That's what John did. He played different roles in the Army to conceal his missions. When he broke his leg,during that mission, he needed a safe cover. I will make the time to share his story later. I want to tell you about this wonderful man. John was my brother, Major Hamilton. I was in Georgia following and caring for my brother while also concealing who I was. There were reasons to do so. Now he is gone. I can say more about his bravery. He was not a coward, Major. He was scared as any human being, but he was not a coward. My husband is taking care of things and will bring the remains back home. My understanding is that his body was unrecognizable. Quintin was given the chain with John's identification that was found near a charred body. Quintin will bring back the remains so that we can properly say goodbye and put him beside our grandmother's resting place. That's all I know right now.

Lacey looked over at her Aunt who stood with Mr. Godfrey-looking somberly in a black dress she also borrowed from her sister for the trip. "We are safe with Mr. Godfrey." Lacey looked up at Doctor Hamilton and asked, "What was your mission prior to our train arriving?"

"I was going to a town north of here. But I'm doubting that I will go now."

"Go, sir, don't miss your train." Lacey raised her chin and looked out through her veil with her steel gray-colored eyes. "Meet the ones that are waiting on you. Some maybe on your calendar, but there may be someone else that is waiting. Pease be there. You will carry John's spirit of joy and determination to care for people. Please do this for John. He had a great respect for what you did for the wounded in the field hospitals. He told me what you did, even for those you knew would die. You gave them dignity. I don't want you to lose your purpose, Gabriel. John wouldn't want that either."

Gabriel held back an emotion that was held tight in his chest. "For John and for you I will go. I will come back in the city in a couple of days. Here, I will give you a card. My solicitor can reach if you need anything."

"That you." Lacey turned toward the Captain. "Marcus Mc-Daniel, you've been away too long. John would want you to refresh yourself, not stand hovering over two ladies in mourning dresses. You've seen all that in the streets of the towns and villages you've traveled in since the war started. Be off with you and buy some of those flowers you passed by on the corner. The stand is next to the barber's. Your beard may have worked well to keep you warm in your tent, but you' are home now and ladies don't like that scratchy stuff when you come close."

"Yes, Lacey dear. I will do as your say. But you send me a message if you need anything." Marcus tapped his heart and gave Lacey a hug."

"Be gone with you both now. I won't keep Mr. Godfrey waiting another moment"

Gabriel watched Lacey walk away. Her dress was slightly too large, which made her look slightly unkempt. It was most likely a hand-me-down from the Clarks where she was staying. She would not have planned to wear a widow's garment to travel in. It *didn't suit her. It never would. The* vivacious *little* nymph wearing *denim and cotton suited her* best, *Gabriel thought. The wild child who rode pepper with her hair pulled under an English cap and* soothed horses *with sugar cubes was the Lacey he wanted to remember. John, how did you pull it off? You never let on that you were anything more than an aid-to-camp, always working to help somebody. For* you, my comrade, *I will take you with me. Your* life's *mission has somehow* become entangled *with mine. When you found me on the mountain road, you had a* broken leg, *but I had a broken heart and didn't even know it.*

"Please sir, give the man a few more second he'll be ready to get on the train in just a minute." Marcus waved his long arm and big hand in Gabriel's direction."

The gruff looking man looked sternly said back. "The man needs to get on the train now or he can catch the next one."

"Sir, just give him a moment. See, he's coming this way."

"You better make it quick, Hamilton, because I'm not taking a shiner for you."

"Okay, I'm ready," said Gabriel as he made it to the train's door. Marcus looked at Gabriel, but Gabriel was fearful of what he would hear.

"She's not calling you to stay, my friend," said Marcus with empathy, but with firmness.

Gabriel looked back at Lacey as she moved along the platform with her aunt. "I know."

"You won't find it here if it's not the right time or the right person."

Gabriel gave his friend a big pat on the back. He wasn't comfortable having a vulnerable side of his show. "I'm going. Okay?"

"When you come back, you look me up. I'll be here for the next ten days. Then I will head back to Washington."

Chapter 11

Searching

The next day, Gabriel visited with his contact at the academy. The meeting went well, but Gabriel didn't feel the excitement he thought he would feel just a week ago when he set out for the trip to New York. Perhaps the ghosts of those who once walked the campus walked beside him as he passed through the common areas where they had previously trod in life forms. Gabriel needed some fresh air after his meetings, so he took the road that passed along the mountain ridge and the river below. It reminded him somewhat of the high gaps in Georgia. He stopped the carriage at a pullout for several minutes. He shared part of his water with the horse and gave him nibbles of the apple that his aunt had put in a basket as a snack. The clopping of the fast-paced rider coming along the same direction that he had just came broke the silence. Gabriel grabbed the reins just in case the horse became spooked.

"Dr. Hamilton!" A boy's voice rang out. "I have a message for you!" A young rider came galloping towards Gabriel.

Gabriel recognized the boy as being one of the Clarks' sons. "Jasper, is something wrong? Is someone ill?"

"No sir, but your aunt received this telegram earlier. She wanted you to see it right away. She thought I might find you sooner on my horse."

"Thank you, Jasper. Let me look at it. Well, it's from my friend Marcus." Gabe thought *that's rather worrisome. Why would Marcus want me in the morning ?* "Thank you Jasper. You caught me just in time for me to pick up a ticket today. Here's some change for your trouble." Gabe thought for a few moments and carried out his plan. He briefly stopped at his aunt and uncle's home, which was on the way. Then headed for the train station. He was fortunate to gain access to the first train and sent a message to his friend at the telegraph office before he headed back to his lodging for the night. This time, he would take the lower road and move at a faster pace.

The sun was fading in the west, shrouding his eyes as he pulled into the lane. Gabriel was quick to dismount from the carriage and prepare his uncle's trusty horse for rest. He let the horse loose in the small fenced in area. The horse came back to the gate to nuzzle his nose one more time into Gabriel's pocket. "One more and that is all, or my uncle will never let me take you again," he said to the horse. Gabriel quickly grabbed his belongings and headed for the kitchen door so as not to track them in from the stables.

"There you are!" Gabriel's aunt responded when she heard the steps on the back porch. She of the kitchen with a big smile. Put your boots right here by the door and slip on a pair of these moccasins. Your uncle makes them from the cow hides after we take one of our cows to butcher in the fall. They make the softest house slippers."

Gabriel took off his heavy boots and put the soft tan slippers on, as his aunt suggested. "Thank you. They fit well."

"I thought they might. I was hoping you would be back for supper this evening as well. I made your father's favorite chess pie. But there is a blueberry cobbler on standby, just in case you prefer fruit pies instead."

"Both are my favorites, Aunt Arline, so I will enjoy either. Thank you for sending Jasper. I booked tomorrow's train. I'm just hoping that something is not wrong. My friend Marcus wouldn't have sent a message unless it was important. I had planned to return because of the service for Mr. Martin tomorrow anyway. I told you about his tragic accident." Gabriel walked in and pulled a chair up to the table after pouring himself some coffee that was on the stove, still hot and smelling fresh.

"Yes, such a sad story. I wish we could have kept you a few more days and fixed you up with one of our darling young ladies at church."

Gabriel smiled. "Perhaps Marcus has gotten me out of jam just in time!" Gabriel gave a smile to his aunt.

"Oh my! A handsome young man like you and not married. You will be the talk of the town. I can see all the ladies running over the other to meet you if you settle around here."

"I need to make my fortune first, Aunt Arline."

"Well, that too, I suppose. Did you find the meeting interesting today?"

"Interesting, yes. I don't think it's calling for me as one of my friends puts it. However, I am a practical person, and I will have to settle down with an offer soon. I am rather eager to get back to work."

"You'll know when it's time." His aunt said and pinched his cheek like a young lad.

"That's what they say. Where's Uncle Winston?"

"He'll be home shortly. He closes the bank around four, and then will stay an extra hour to lock things up. You'll see he will pull up in his carriage at 4:55 PM sharp. Supper served promptly in the dining room at 6:00 PM. Why don't you relax until dinner? That will free me up to put everything on platters and get them ready for the sideboard. I let the housekeeper go home earlier since she had been here cooking with me all day. She has her own family to tend to as well. I am blessed when she comes to help on Mondays and Wednesdays. Winston and I are a lot simpler than many of the surrounding folks. We like the quiet time in the evenings. She tapped Gabriel's hand. "But we love our visitors too. Your father should visit us more. We don't miss the entertainments of the big city now that we are older. The spring and summer months give us enough excitement when many of our old friends visit. The Clarks have been one of the dearest friends we've had here. Perhaps there will be another time you will get to meet them. They always have interesting guests at their dinner parties. They may be heading out on the same train tomorrow, as they were relatives of sorts with the Thaxtons." Gabriel's aunt stopped for a moment and looked outside the kitchen window. Yes, there's your uncle now."

"Great! Let me go out and help him with the horse and carriage. I will bring him in before dusk."

"Ah, you may try, but it's hard to change the ways of that dear, sweet man."

Gabriel shared a comforting evening with his aunt and uncle. The small pleasures that come from being around those that truly share a bond of affection for one another is soothing. Around the fires at the camps, there was a sense of brotherhood too, in a different way. Those brothers were not always blood relatives, chosen from different backgrounds and belief systems, all pulled together out of duty and purpose. One's survival depended on each other. Only God had the wisdom to know when it was time for someone to go home. For those who were not called yet, Gabriel had fought to keep them alive. *I still feel the warrior inside somewhere wanting to heal my brothers.* He would continue looking. *He must belong somewhere.*

The next morning Gabriel was one of the early ones waiting for the first train to Philadelphia by way of New York. The train was full by the time the conductor had closed the door. He was happy to have a window seat today, and those around him were not too chatty. After an hour or so, he decided to take out a medical journal he had brought with him to read. The man sitting diagonally looked over for a moment and initiated a conversation.

"I see you're reading a journal regarding surgery. May I ask you if you are a physician?"

Gabriel looked up and responded. "Yes, I am a surgeon. I actually just left my position in the military."

"How interesting." The gentleman from a state out west was also a surgeon. In fact, his oldest son was too. He had been in New York looking at some new techniques that he wanted to take back to the small clinic where he was working.

Gabriel could feel the passion in the man's voice as he spoke about what he was doing. It was a small practice, but there was a spark in the man's voice. Gabriel gravitated to sounds of the man's voice. He felt the importance of this man's purpose.

"I had a similar interest when I was reading about this surgeon who was working on developing reconstruction surgery for the men injured from gunshot and shrapnel wounds. It sounded like pretty amazing work. I was still working in a field hospital off the James and then later in the hospitals around Washington," Gabriel responded.

"I've heard my brother talk about stuff like that. We don't see that kind of injury very much where we are, but we definitely are interested in discovering the best ways to do things. I've been to

France a couple of times to learn some techniques. We are also learning how to be operationally more efficient as we go along. "It's just plain common sense to think of the patient experience. We are not all saws and butchers. Some of us really want to heal. I read a story once that Joseph heal people with some sort of ointment with honey. Can you believe the ancient Egyptians were using smarter techniques than generations that followed?"

"I would agree. I learned a lot from the Indian tribes that remained in Georgia while I was there. I believe there is a science in some of those ancient ways. We just haven't discovered it yet."

"Yes. I love the adventure of pressing on and finding better ways to do something. I'm just practical too. The results are what is important to me. I would love for you to meet my brother. I think you and he would hit it off."

"Thank you. Most of my studies came from my education in Philadelphia. I have some friends that I studied with, and they have done a lot of great work while we were at war. I want to do something worthwhile too. Medicine has really changed in this century. I want to be part of that change."

"I'm going to write my contact information here. Please keep in touch when you get back home. I think we have a lot in common," said the young doctor. I am catching another train when we reach the city. When you get back home, don't forget me. Write and tell me what you decide to do with your experience."

"Thank you." Gabriel exchanged his contract information as well. By the time the train docked at the train station, Gabriel quickly departed to catch the next train that would take him home. He felt lighter after that train ride than he had all week. Yes, he wanted some of what that young man had. He wanted to feel alive again, or maybe he wanted to feel alive for the first time. No, that's not true either. There were moments in the last year when he thought he felt it, but he was afraid to acknowledge that there was something new happening to him. McDaniel's telegram sounded important so He would address it soon enough. When the train came to a holt Gabriel was quick to grab his things and walk off the train. Sure enough, his friend was waiting.

"I'm over here Gabriel. I've got a carriage waiting. No sense in you staying in a lonely hotel when my home is not so far, and we have plenty of room to keep you."

"Thank you. I will take you up on that given I've been on a train for over eight hours and I'm just not up to hiring a carriage and hunting down a room for the night."

"I thought you might feel that way. Let's get out of here and head home," Gabriel's friend responded.

"Do you know if Martin's body has made it back yet?"

"Yes, I saw the train arrive while I was waiting for yours. It was interesting that Major Thaxton was on the same train in a special car along with guess who?"

"I don't know!" Gabriel replied.

"It was Grant in full uniform. I don't know the significance, but the general was there."

"Do you know where he is staying?"

"No, he left with two other men in uniform and scurried away in a closed carriage as soon as he arrived. Major Thaxton stayed and watched them drape the casket. He helped carry the box off the train. A hearse took the box from there and Major Thaxton got in a carriage and followed down the street. I don't know if anyone was in the carriage, but it had a driver. Do you think that John Martin was more than a private?"

"You would think I would know the answer, but I don't," Gabriel said. "I think he was more than an aide in my camp. Everything points to him knowing so much more. I first met John Martin along a mountain road near a battlefield. He wound from a fall left him with a leg injury, so I requested that our regiment bring him on our way to meet up with Sherman's massive columns. Prior to that, we had orders to leave our position, which was on higher ground. I couldn't figure out the importance of why we were even there. Ordered to some far away isolated mountain gap was my punishment for a misstep I had had made in Washington. Maybe it wasn't at all. Private Martin became my assistant while he was recovering, and he just stayed with me the rest of the time until I spent the last few weeks back in Washington prior to me leaving the Army. The field hospital that I was in first had been taken down after the surrender of Lee and his army. Martin stayed with me. I didn't need him anymore when I went to the hospital near the White house. He ended up being reassigned just before I received my discharge papers. I was more intrigued by the special courier during all those months. I never gave John a thought of his true purpose. He never caused an upset or made a mistake with anything he did."

"The courier?"

"The special courier that came around. Don't you remember?" Gabriel asked.

"I don't know what you're talking about, Gabriel. I never had contact with a special courier."

"Stop that. Don't put on that mask now? There was a courier that brought us supplies at the camp and messages in pouches. The pouches were made of tanned leather."

"I never saw anything like that come to camp," McDaniel replied.

"When I was in Georgia, the pouches arrived in camp for the colonel. We got orders to move on from the gap, because of the information in the pouch!"

"Gabriel, I'm not saying you didn't see a pouch. I'm just saying my camp never saw a courier that brought a pouch. Our supplies always came in by wagon, usually from the train that was making a stop." McDaniel responded.

"You are serious, aren't you? You can tell me that you have orders to not say anything, but please don't say you never saw or heard of a special courier bringing information in a deerskin pouch."

"I swear to you I never received information from a deerskin pouch or anything else except a box or package with the army stamp on it. Information relayed to us typically came through a telegraph we had in the camp."

"John Martin was just a young man. Why would he be more than a private?" Gabriel asked.

"Gabriel, I think that's where you need to stop thinking. If he had wanted you to know, he would have told you. Was he ever out of turn or looking into your things like a spy would be?"

"No, never!" Gabriel responded.

"Okay, then he wasn't a confederate spy trying to find your position or your stash. Maybe he was trying to get information and supplies through. It was difficult-to-reach some of our units because of geography or because the enemy was so close."

"He was my aide to camp, my personal assistant!"

"Was he really?" McDaniel responded somberly.

"Major Thaxton and General Sherman worked closely together from the time Grant was still in Tennessee. I wouldn't think that Grant would attend a private's funeral. I'm realizing that Martin was more than that. I think I've been a pawn in a game of chess. I've been moved around the board of battle by someone else's hand. Pieces continue to be knocked off the board. I'm not sure why I'm still in the game."

"I can't give insight into that deep thought, my friend, but I can lead us to a splendid dinner and a clean bed. Come to my home tonight. My wife's been keeping me from her fresh blueberry pies until I bring you home. I cannot resist the thought anymore of sitting down with that fruit pie teasing my tongue and then filling my gullet."

"You are talking like a pirate now, but I'm ready. Let's get to your home and let me think about this some more. By the way, what was the importance of getting me on the first train? I thought something might be wrong." Gabriel carried his bag and followed his friend.

"Did you meet anyone special on the train today?"

"Special is a vague word, McDaniel. Can you be more specific?"

"Did you meet another physician on the train today?" asked Marcus.

"Yes, I did. I wrote his name down. It was something like Bayo or Payo?"

"You did you get along with him?"

"Yes. He was very interesting as a someone to talk with on the train. How did you know I would meet him?"

"I knew he was leaving today on the early train. We have mutual friends, you see. I wanted to be sure you and he were on the same train this morning."

"Why is that friend?"

"Because he's part of your future."

"How do you know that? Do you read tea leaves or something else when you are not sawing on bones?"

"I just know things. I know you met him. That's fate. I think your bed must have been very hard last night. You are very stiff and ugly this morning," quipped Gabriel's friend.

"I've seen your pattern before. Are you attempting to influence me again? Is one of your wise sayings about ready to come out of that mouth of yours like "It's not time.""

"Ah, so you were listening to me the other day. That's a relief. Listen to me about this too, as I think there is a connection between you. I have more information to back up this kernel of wisdom. I met his son a year ago. We've been in touch ever since. I sent a telegram to him a message when I knew you were here. He told me his father was visiting a friend after some time in Boston. He told me the train he would be on. I just put you two on the same train coming back. No harm meeting another colleague."

"He seemed very interesting. So you know his son. It's a small world. What is he like?" Gabe asked.

"Very smart and gifted. He has a genuine hunger to learn. There's a special place in history for that family. I will bet the dollar in my pocket."

"You're probably right. I'm feeling rather like taking up residence here, Marcus. After all, I've seen so far, I feel like this feels like home to me. I would like to stay near my colleagues. Yes, I've never really said that out loud, but yes, that is what I want to do. I started seeing the needs while I was in the field hospitals. That is what fires my insides up."

"Well, if that is what you want to do then, you have my support, and I know there are people who would support you in this city. I like where your thoughts are going, my friend" Marcus directed Gabriel to his carriage. "Let's go to my home. I'm sure my wife is waiting for our arrival."

"All right, Marcus, that sounds good." Gabriel was exhausted, and he was happy to have somewhere to go to be around friends. He knew he wasn't worth his salt in conversation this evening, but he could at least wash up and have a safe place to sleep for the night. That would allow his mind to process the recent events in a healthy way. There was so much riding on making good choices. He needed a quiet spot to lay his concerns down off his shoulders in a safe place, a place where only he and God could talk.

The next few days were a blur of activity. The ceremony at the church for Private Martin was simple, but elegant. Gabriel had few words to share with the family, as people were always surrounding them. Quintin took the time to give Gabriel a quick update on his plans before heading back to his regiment. They exchanged information on how to contact one another. He would stay in touch. He found himself still tied to the one who met him in Dunbar's Gap.

Chapter 12

Coming Home Wounded

Months had pasted since the day at the John Martin's funeral. Gabriel quickly engulfed himself in building his practice and becoming an active medical team member at the local medical school. It felt good to reconnect with old friends. He had written Lacey a few lines regarding his plans for the clinic. Her responses were always welcome. They were always supportive. It had been almost a year since he had left Washington as an officer in the military. Now he was back near where he had been before the war. *So many things have* changed, *Gabe thought.* He had written Lacey a few lines regarding his plans for the clinic. Her responses were always welcomed and where supportive. He wanted to visit her again, but wanted to be respectful of her period of mourning. Besides, he had so many new things to be involved in now. His life was full of purpose. At least Gabriel hoped it did. There were no more social parties every night and heavy drinking like his first days in Washington. This Friday, Gabriel's plan was to spend his day at the clinic all day. Since the weather was warm and the days were longer, he decided to walk this morning as the clinic was just a few blocks away from the town home he was renting. He had looked at his list of patients he was to see. He noted a new patient on the list at the very end of the day. That was a curious thing, as those patients were prioritized before 1:00. Gabriel assumed someone needed to be put in an emergency and put the list on the clipboard. The day went as expected. The nurse was rather vague with symptoms when Dr. Hamilton asked about the new patient's history. She excused herself to another room as he passed, stating, "The patient wanted to share the symptoms only with the doctor."

Dr. Hamilton shrugged his shoulders and turned the knob to let himself into the room. He dashed in and closed the room without scanning the adjoining area that connected the consulting room and his office. Gabriel laughed. "I think we need to isolate this patient. This is surely a case of the dreaded measles!" Gabriel smiled. He looked carefully at the patient in front of him. "So, what is it this time?"

"Come see." She turned her cheek from cheek to cheek. Then, she opened her hand to show pieces of red candy in her hand."

Gabriel walked closer and wiped a speck from her face. "It was more believable the first time." He smiled back warmly. "Lacey, what has brought you here today?"

She blushed slightly and said, "Actually, it was my grandfather right here" She pointed to the man who sat nonchalantly in the chair.

"We came this way so that we could invite you to our home for dinner. I fear you are staying away from calling us on purpose. So my grandfather thought we would reach out with a more forceful approach. It also gave me an opportunity to see how well you are getting along."

"What?"

"We came for you. I was hoping you would come to our home and spend dinner with my grandfather and me." We have a carriage outside waiting. We can stop by your home, and you can pick up an overnight bag if you please so that you don't have to go back in the dark. My grandfather has been missing you."

"This sounds a bit like kidnapping," Dr Hamilton said with humor in his voice.

"Not at all. You can say no. But we would love for you to come, and you are always so busy. I thought I might squeeze in dinner as I had already asked around, discreetly, of course, if you had any known obligations. I have friends too, you see."

"In that case, I may have to set up a surveillance system. But regards to the first matter. You are right, I had no dinner plans this evening and I would very much enjoy the company."

Mr. Thaxton spoke up. "My granddaughter is correct. I have been missing our chess game and discussions after dinner. It's been several weeks now since you have visited. We feel you need a break from all this once in a while."

"Then it is settled. When can we leave?" Lacey responded.

"Give me 10 minutes to finish my notes. You can stay here and use the basin to clear those candied freckles off you face. I will come and get you. This chair should be comfortable enough by the window. I will open the blinds so you can watch people. I'll be back in just a few minutes, and I will let my nurse and secretary go home. They will enjoy not having to wait around for me."

As precisely as Gabriel said, all three individuals were loading into the private carriage within the next 10 minutes. The sensory experience of the 19th century surrounded them as he rode with the Lacey and her grandfather through the city streets. The clopping sounds of hooves tickled the ears. His eyes brightened watching the painted small boat shaped wagons with red wheels and blue wooden sides. Heard were the tinkling of bells several blocks down as the specially bred horses pulled their cargo down to the docs or out to the Pike, which would lead them across the state. Perhaps they would stop at the stone inn that Gabriel and his father had stopped at as a teenager. Gabriel had missed the simple symbols of home during his days on the battlefield. The clinic was several blocks from the Thaxton's home of the river and Gabriel's home was on the way at the midpoint. Gabriel was thankful for his friends coming to his rescue and pulling him back into a life away from work. Gabriel grabbed a couple of things from his home and quickly jumped back into the carriage. Once at the Thaxton's, a welcoming feeling left Gabriel comfortable among friends. Ushered to the back porch, Gabriel observed a breeze and the fragrance of gardenias was in the air.

Lacey took the role of hostess and poured Gabriel and her grandfather a glass of refreshment. I enjoyed it with a wedge of lemon and a teaspoon of honey. See if this is to your liking.

Gabriel smiled back. "Yes, that would be fine. I'm sure I will enjoy any way you fix it. Just sitting here and taking in the scenery is a treat."

Lacey smiled back and "Excused herself to the kitchen to check on things." When all was ready, they all set themselves around a table that had been on the table covered with a colorful cloth. Thoughtfully platters of food placed on the table with fresh flowers in the center of the table. The meal was ready. Conversation around a dinner was the perfect way to end the week, they all agreed.

Gabriel looked up a few times and looked towards the hedge at the back of the yard. The alley was behind a small stable that stood at the back of the property. He thought he caught something moving but could not see through the thick hedge.

"Gabriel, has something stolen your attention?" Lacey asked as she watched Gabriel's eyes wonder again to the back of the property."

"No, I just keep catching something from the corner of my eye and I'm not sure what it is."

"What is it you're looking at?" Mr. Thaxton asked.

"It's nothing. I just keep seeing movement at the left of the stable. I thought it was a horse."

"Horses, you say? That's odd," Mr. Thaxton remarked.

Lacey got up out of her chair immediately. She snuck a couple of cubes of sugar in her side pocket and immediately head down the steps and into the direction that Gabriel was looking at."

"Lacey, hold on. Wait for me.!" Gabriel responded.

Mr. Thaxton also got up from his chair and started walking in the same direction. Something was going on around the barn.

Lacey walked to a gate to the back of the lot where the hedgerow was. By this time, Gabriel had caught up.

"Let's go slowly, Lacey. We don't know what it is yet. Let me go first. You stay here and let me go take a peak first." The others lost Gabriel from sight as he moved beyond gate and on the other side of the row of holly trees. Gabriel pulled the gate and walked into the alley. He looked down to the right and saw nothing. When he looked to the left, he was stunned. "Oh, my word! Come here, Pepper. Don't be afraid. Why are you here, my friend?" Gabriel patted the horse's neck to calm her down. He looked around to look for clues for Jake or evidence of what was transpiring.

While Gabriel was checking beyond the hedge, Lacey heard sounds from inside the stable. She slowly opened the door and felt someone pull her inside. She gasped when she felt someone take her by the waist and put a hand over her mouth.

"I won't hurt you. Just be quiet," a male voice said to her in a quiet voice.

Lacey wrestled and eventually gave an elbow hit to the ribs, which forced the intruder to let her go. She yelled out. "Help!" She immediately lunged towards the pitchfork against the wall and turned around to the assailant to attack.

The man had cried out in pain and picked up a shovel to protect himself from the impending assault.

Then she shrieked and cried out. "Oh, my God! John! She put the pitchfork down as her assailant mirrored her actions.

The intruder looked dazed for a moment. "You called me John." His hands fell away from Lacey's body. He closed his eyes for a moment. "Is my name John?" He then dropped to his knees and put his hands up to his ears as if he was hearing something and trying to close out the sound.

Lacey watched the young man melt in front of her. "Yes, John. I am your sister, Lacey. Don't you know me?"

By then, the side door slammed open, and Mr. Thaxton rushed inside with a hoe that had been in the garden.

"Stop! Please don't hurt John!" Lacey cried out to her grandfather.

Mr. Thaxton immediately put the hoe down and looked at the man crouched down on the floor of the barn. "My God, is this true? A miracle has happened. Thank God above. John, let me help you up, son." Mr. Thaxton could see that John was in some distress by the expression on his face. The old man crouched down to the young man and touched his shoulders.

John, are you in any pain? Mr. Thaxton put both hands on the young man's shoulders. He could tell that he was frail and had lost muscle in his arms, but he saw now open wounds on the surface.

"Who's John?" the young man asked. He's eyes showed confusion.

Mr. Thaxton spoke gently. "I'm your grandfather, John. Your name is John Martin. Lacey is your sister. You are home? We thought you were dead, but through a miracle, God brought your home."

Gabriel opened the doors to the stable a few seconds later. He immediately came to the opening to assess the situation. "Lacey, are you alright? Is Jake in here with you?"

Lacey turned to face Gabriel with tears in her eyes. She moved away, so that Gabriel had a better view of who she was looking at. She smiled with tears running down her face, speechless to say more.

Gabriel saw the confusion in the young man's face and whispered, "Oh my God." Gabriel could feel the nudging of a soft wet nose against his shoulder and knew that Pepper was acknowledging the presence of a long-lost friend, a friend who appeared to be in danger. Pepper continued to push Gabriel closer into the barn. "John, I am Doctor Hamilton, Major Hamilton. Do you remember me?"

The young man sat on the floor of the barn. He resorted to holding his knees up to his chest and calm rocking to calm his inner tempest. He attempted to answer the familiar voice in his head.

"My name is John. She said you were coming down the road and you would help me, and she told me not to be scared. My leg is hurting. I think it's broken."

Lacey took John's hand and cried. Through the tears, she added, "Yes, John, your leg was hurt. But it is better now. The doctor is here, and he will keep you safe. Dr. Hamilton is here. Do you remember Major Hamilton?" Lacey responded in a soothing voice.

John was still confused, but something was liberating him from the darkness. The voices seemed familiar. *Where did he know them from?* "Dr. Hamilton, I'm coming with you." John spoke at last.

"Yes John, I'm here too, along with Lacey and you grandfather? We are glad you made it home. It seems you might have been in an accident or been ill. But you are safe now. We are all here to help you."

John stood up slowly. He was afraid to move in any direction. In his mind, he was still lost.

Gabriel chimed in. "John can go to the mess tent with me. Follow me up to the house. I suspect you're hungry," said Dr. Hamilton, trying to meet John wherever his mind was at the moment. I bet you're hungry."

"Yes, I am, sir. But I'll eat with the other soldiers."

"Not today, John. You'll eat with the officers. We are all up at the house together. You can come with me. We can all be together."

"Thank you, sir."

"I'm glad you're home. How long has it been since you ate something?"

John shook his head. "I don't remember, sir. I remember being on a boat. There were nurses and doctors around me. I didn't want to go with them. I ran, sir." John sat still for a moment and looked around. "I am thirsty. Could I have some water?"

"Absolutely," Gabriel turned toward Lacey. "Can get John some water. Bring it in one of the tin cups, just in case. No glass. Walk calmly so that nothing triggers John's fears. We can wait here until you get back," said Gabriel.

"Yes, of course." Lacey went into the house and grabbed the requested item from the kitchen. She moved as fast as she could to return.

Just then, a middle-aged woman came dashing through the hedges. "My dears, what is going on? I saw Dr. Hamilton's. Then I heard the commotion. Is someone ill?"

Mr. Thaxton let out a sigh when he heard the voice of his sister. "All is well," he responded. "Please keep your voice down."

"Can I help?" was the voice of a middle-aged woman running full speed in her day dress and house slippers. "I watched the commotion from the window."

Mr. Thaxton responded with a calm, firm voice. "John has come back, but he is injured. We are helping him get up to the porch. Now sister, please do not alarm him."

Mrs. Jennings instantly broke out in tears of joy. She saw her brother raise his hand to request quiet. "Maybe he would like something to eat. Something light think would be best. I have a pot on the fire with some chicken and dumplings. Oh yes, let me run and bring some over, just in case he is hungry. John always loved chicken and dumpling. Yes, that's what I will bring for over." She picked up her skirts and ran back through the hedges."

Lacey held the cup to John's lips and let him take a sip. She then gave the cup to Dr. Hamilton.

Gabriel responded with, "Thank you," and steadied the cup as John took sips of water.

Lacey said, "I'll get his bed ready and get some water for a bath. If the clothes in his closet won't work, we'll use something of Quintin's."

Another voice was heard outside of the barn. "There's the wagon! Pepper, why did you run off like that? What is going on here?" said a voice that Gabriel had heard before.

"Jake, is that you?" said Gabriel.

"Yes, it is Dr. Hamilton."

"Come here Jake. We are all in the barn, but you can help us move John to the house. Then you can tell us what happened."

"I am so sorry. Pepper and the wagon disappeared while I was opening up the stable at your place. I tried to run, following the wagon. I had to stop a couple of times and ask if anyone saw it come by as I lost sight of him a couple of times. Is everything okay, sir?" the young man replied.

"Yes. The timing of your delivery was perfect. Pepper came here when I wasn't at home. He brought John here, it seems." Just then, another voice came from outside the barn.

"I have some soup," cried out Mrs. Jennings. The women scurried to the porch. Everyone was starting to move John in that direction. "How is John?" Mrs. Jennings asked her brother. She could see now that John was not fully aware of his surroundings. He's injured somehow. But he's home now, and that was all that mattered.

Mr. Thaxton responded. "Thank you. We are all fine, but we need to care for John at the moment, sister. Let's keep it between us all until I can alert his brother. Our priority is to care for his health and mind. I am sure he needs some recovery time before he is up for company."

"Well, of course, Oh my angels, John is alive, and he is here!" cried out Mrs. Jennings.

"Yes, that is what I said," said Mr. Thaxton.

"Oh Lacey, what joy for you," Mrs. Jennings cried out. "Let me go back over to the house. I am going to open my late husband's closet and have his finest washed and pressed and send them over to you tomorrow. I knew there would be a joyous occasion that would make me open those drawers again. We will get John well in no time with the gifted help of Dr. Hamilton." She threw general kisses in the air and scurried back to her yard, where she briskly ran up the steps and flew into the house across the hedge.

John stood quietly, not knowing how to respond to this new situation where everyone else seemed to know their part, but his role was confusing.

"Don't worry, my son. My sister's intentions are always good," said Mr. Thaxton.

"Grandpa!" Lacey said with tears running down her face, but a joy sparking from her eyes.

"I don't want to scare John off now. My sister can be a little big on drama. But she has a big heart and wants to share it with everyone. For now, she can help by working from the distance at her own home so we can keep things calm for John," Mr. Thaxton said with a wink and a mischievous-looking grin.

John continued to show signs of confusion. He blurted out in distress. "Major Hamilton, a pouch came for you today."

Gabriel turned his attention to John. Using a gentle voice, he responded. "Yes, John, I received that pouch. Did you know what was in it?"

I didn't look in the pouch, sir. I have orders, sir. I can't tell you where the courier went." John showed distress and Dr. Hamilton did not want to create more of a situation, so he tried to calm his emotions down. "John, you did the right thing. Now let's take care of your belly. I'm sure you are hungry."

"I saw it by accident when you tried to move the pouch to your chest. It peaked through. I didn't mean to see it, but I knew what it meant."

"I see. Thank you, Private Martin. I want to hear about that very much, but let's take care of you first." Gabriel looked closely at John to attempt to imagine what John must be experiencing right now. Then Gabriel looked at Lacey. He mouthed to her, "It's okay, let's get him up to the house."

Lacey understood and chimed in. "I'm going to walk with you so we can sit down on the porch." Gabriel sat him down and allowed him to try some soup before taking him upstairs.

Lacey quickly walked over to the barn where Pepper was waiting with Jake. She pulled out the sugar from her pockets and shared it with her equine friend. She rubbed her mane and her neck. The Hamilton's farmhand carried Gabriel's package up to the house.

After nourishment and a warm bath. Dr. Hamilton asked Lacey to come with him while he examined John. He appeared to be in reasonable shape, considering what he had presumably gone through the last six months. It was mainly signs of amnesia and behaviors associated with soldiers who have had traumatic events. The anxiousness was present, which might have meant that doctors might have treated him with some form of medication. Gabriel was nervous about giving him anything that wouldn't mix with something that was already in his system and working its way out. Hamilton helped John upstairs. Lacey helped him bath and Dr. Hamilton carefully examined for any medical concerns. John appeared to calm down after that and rested in the half-tester bed that was his growing up. Mr. Thaxton wanted to watch over John for a few hours to make sure he remained sleeping.

Gabriel escorted Lacey to the parlor, where they could talk more. "So that I can help John, tell me a little of his background and then what you and he were doing in the gap," Gabe asked Lacey.

Lacey was willing to share her family history with Gabriel, as he had shown himself to be trustworthy when it concerned her family. The Thaxton and Martin families have been friends for years. With both George Thaxton and Mrs. Martha Martin became widowers many years ago, they married each other, and our families were melted together. My father was Martha's son, my grandmother. He served as a soldier and was working with relocating the Indian tribes into forts until being transported out west. My mother grew up near the area I first met you near the gap of the Georgia mountains. My reportedly was very beautiful and young and my father feared that harm would come to her at the fort or along the way. He protected her by marrying her and brought her to live with his parents until he could leave the military. My mother's parents both died from smallpox while being detained in one of the relocation forts. I have seen a painting of my mother, but I'm told that in life she was even more striking. John came first and then I came a couple of years later. We were very happy growing up. Quintin's mother passed away first. I don't remember her much. Shortly afterward, Grandfather Martin passed away. George and Martha, both widowers, decided to marry. A couple of years later. My parents were both taken away in a storm as they were returning from Savannah by boat. John was ten, and I was eight. We had been spending the summer with our grandparents when the shipwreck accident occurred. Grandfather Thaxton and my grandmother immediately became our guardians. Quintin, John and I became family. George and Martha managed the pharmacy business while John and I were growing up. There were some products the company sold to the military which kept the business making a profit over the years, which allowed John and me a personal income from investment money. My grandfather guided my grandmother to put the funds while we were young, and John and I are both grateful. Our income is not all from the Thaxton's. When I turned a teenager Quintin was away in New York. He came back, and I was sent to finishing school in Boston. When I returned, I was invited to attend a large party with many of Quintin's friends. I think he got a little jealous of the attention I received, and it wasn't long before he proposed. I was perfectly fine with that, as I had worshiped him almost my entire life. He was my knight in shining armor. Don't get me wrong, he has flaws. As the war went on, John felt he needed to do more. I didn't want to be left by either of them, so I came up with ways to support Quintin and John while they were at war."

"I see," said Gabriel.

"I know you want to know more. I can't tell you everything, but I can tell you that I was working to protect John and his mission."

"What about the gap, Lacey?" asked Gabe.

Lacey chose her words carefully. "I was frantic to save my brother when he broke his leg in that ravine in Georgia. He would have been harmed or killed if left out there. I had to find some way to get him out of those woods. I knew your Corp had a doctor and would pass soon. The colonel received secret instructions. He was aware of the consequences of disobeying orders. Your men provided cover and support in transporting and protecting people out of those foothills. It was the best option available. I couldn't take him with me on horseback. We would never have made it to safety."

Gabriel sat quietly for a moment. "Wow, that is a lot to soak in. Thank you for sharing, Lacey. There's a lot more to the story, though. Do you know many of the generals? I'm sure many are acquaintances of Quintin's."

"Yes, and no. I can't say much more. I will say I kept up wherever John was. I knew he would be safe if he was placed as your assistant," Lacey added.

"How did you make that happen?" Gabriel asked in a quiet voice.

"You give me too much power. I can't tell you anything more," Lacey said.

"Would you tell me if you were spies?"

"No, we were not spies. We had a mission that was known by a few."

"Who knew?"

"You know I can't say," Lacey responded.

"You followed me to Virginia from Georgia." Gabriel replied.

"I was caring for my family, but I needed to stay unknown to the masses. I couldn't do what I need to do if the wrong people found me."

"You left me things, messages, and things that I needed."

"Yes, I did. It was the least I could do for you and your men."

"Lacey, I am sorry if I ever put you in a difficult situation. How was I to know you weren't a camp thief, or someone trying to steal camp secrets?"

"I was fulfilling my purpose, and that was all." Lacey knew that was all she would say. That compartment of her life was now closed.

"I'll accept that." Gabe knew it was pointless to go on like this any further. "I will come back in the morning and check on John. I also want to contact someone who might work with John on dealing with stress and the trauma that he must have experienced. It's possible that he may have had an injury to the head that has caused the amnesia. I know there is some literature about people experiencing train wrecks with some behaviors that are somewhat similar. I have to go back and read the sources. I am a doctor trained in surgery. Maybe we need to find a doctor that is trained or has a personal interest in injuries from trauma or head injuries. Let me help you find the help that John needs."

"Yes. Whatever he needs, we will find it. Quintin and grandfather will support anything that is best for John."

"Great! I'm going to say goodbye to your family. I will check in on John in the morning."

"We owe you such a debt of gratitude for all that you've done."

"John deserves the very best. I am doing nothing more than how I would treat any of my men under my command or those wounded in my care. Your work is just beginning, young lady. As a warning, I am telling you that there will be some rough times along with the times of joy ahead. You may become a doctor yet."

"I think I would like that!" said Lacey and walked their guest to the door.

Gabriel left the Thaxton's with mixed emotions and he did not want to show his distress with others at the moment. Jake took the reins while Dr. Hamilton pulled himself up into the wagon. His thoughts were somewhere else as he returned home.

The next morning Gabriel followed up with a call at the Thaxton's and noting all was going well. He left the patient in the caring hands of his family. Gabriel had recommended someone to Lacey to contact to follow up with John's needs. It was in John's best interest to find the specialized support that he needed to make a full recovery. He would let the family with their connections deal with the messy business of who it was they buried several months ago.

Chapter 13

Doctor's Orders

Three months had passed since John Martin had returned home. Gabriel had tried to stay away as much as possible, leaving John in the capable hands of another physician who understood more about these types of injuries and the family. However, he visited John as a friend and previous commander on regular occasions. John had quite a story. He would recover well, Dr Hamilton predicted. His memory was slowing coming back with major details about the accident missing. Gabriel felt the selfish pang of jealousy when John's sister fluttered around the room. In his quiet moments, Gabriel contemplated if Philadelphia was meant for him. It was on one of those occasions while Gabriel was sitting in his library at home. He flinched when he heard the door knocker clang and his housekeeper opening the door. The housekeeper, knowing the visitor, brought the visitor straight to the library.

"Well, look at you, my old friend!" said Gabriel as he saw the bearded face of his friend McDaniel.

"So they let you come home!" Gabriel teased as he went to shake his old friend's hand.

"Yes, I decided I would try my luck outside of a uniform. I think I kind of like it so far. I hope I'm not taking up too much of your time. I did not have time to send a notice of my arrival."

"I would have put someone else to cover if I was too busy!" Gabe said while leading his old friend.

"I went to see the Thaxtons earlier today. It is extraordinary that John is alive and that he has recovered almost fully," said McDaniels.

"Yes, I will stop in now and then. He's doing well, remembering most of what has happened to date. There's a few things he might never recall. I suspect that's natural. He remembers being on that train and getting off, but then everything goes blank. I suspect he's had a blow to the head. Why his name tags were found on another body that was unrecognizable, I'm not sure. It was enough information to make Quintin think he really was dead."

Dr. McDaniel took a swig of the scotch from his glass. "Does Lacey ever say much?"

Gabriel looked at his friend somberly. "About what?"

"You know. When you two first met. Back in the gap?"

Gabe tapped his glass. "No, she has told me the reason for her being in Georgia was to follow her family. Nothing really more than that." An uncomfortable pause passed, and Gabriel continued. "Quintin's coming home for good soon. He's a good man. He's been talking about getting involved in investing in medical equipment, building facilities and stuff like that. I don't know. He has a lot on his plate."

"That sounds like him. What are you up to these days?" asked Gabriel's friend.

"You know, I'm building the practice and teaching at the college one day a week. Surgeons keep unpredictable hours, you know."

"That is the truth," said McDaniel.

"Lacey wants me to help her become a doctor. She wants to be involved in medical care for children. There's already a children's hospital in town that started a few years ago. She doesn't need me for that. I don't really work with children. They scare me too much. Those little pudgy things, rolling on the floor, putting anything in their mouths they can get their hands on. That is much too distressing for me. Quintin can certainly help her make the right connections if Lacey wants to pursue her idea of medicine."

"Yes, I'm sure the family has connections. He's not a doctor, though," McDaniel added.

"Should I trade my saws and clamps for something a little smaller and less scary, just to be here crutch? I think that would not go well with my darker personality, who prefers to play poker with the men on Saturday night occasionally or better yet, my fondness for brandy when there's a nip in the fall air. Besides, she doesn't need me for that. She has the talent. If she has the desire, no one can stop her." replied Gabriel.

"I'm not disagreeing with a word you said. You have some connections in the city and at the college. I'm sure you could help her connect with the right people who can explain the process."

"You sound like my father now." The two men continued to ramble on for another hour. There was a lot they had shared while they were part of the medical corp. Now that the war was over and they had gone their separate ways, there was still a connection that was as deep as brotherly attachment.

McDaniel eventually felt a tug in his heart that he wanted to ease. It was time to change the subject. Not finding the right way to blend the conversation with the previous topics. McDaniel took an off-topic route in the conversation. "There is an invitation for an evening of entertainment at the Van Dorn's home next Friday. I highly recommend that you come with my wife and me. There will be some very interesting people at this gathering. Some you know already, and some unfamiliar faces too. I have to get my feet wet in society again now that I'm no longer in the military. I married above me, so I have to get used to doing these things for her. How she picked me out of the litter, I'm not sure," replied McDaniel.

"I didn't know that we ranked that high in the society. Thanks for the heads up. I don't believe I know the family hosting the gathering. I most likely will politely turn down the invitation. Any reason why I was I was invited?" Gabe responded with less than moderate interest.

"That's why I am here. I was told that you would be your response. You probably have mutual friends that will be there, that kind of thing. I think word is getting out about your work with those magical hands of yours. Was there something about an almost ruptured appendix recently?" James McDaniel was not one to take a refusal lightly.

"Not that story again. I can't take all the credit. Classic symptoms and routine surgical technique on a healthy patient otherwise. I was present when the young man was having symptoms. I am happy it worked out well. I'm humbled that anyone would even think it was worth talking about."

"Be that as it may, the family is grateful and a relative of the Van Dorns. You are making a name for yourself."

"Well, I will check with the housekeeper when I get home. If an invitation arrives, I promise to check my calendar. However, don't count on me coming. With all respect to the host and hostess, I think I might be a very boring guest," Gabriel replied.

"You see, my friend. That is what I'm talking about. You're in grief. You saw the loss of life and property in the war. I'm afraid you heart was lost to someone who was never meant for you. Now you are in need to put that energy that's built up. It needs a place to go, Gabriel. I am worried about you."

"I'm fine. McDaniel, just fine."

"Okay, if you say so. I've done my duty. " McDaniel picked up his hat and prepared to depart. "Come on back from the war, Gabriel. Someone needs you at home." McDaniel started for the door.

Gabriel stood up with a stoic expression. He walked his friend to the entrance. "Come back James. Maybe I will be a bit more entertaining next time."

"You are fine as you are, Gabe. Please think about next week. My wife enjoys your company."

"Thank you. I'll see what I can do." Gabe watched his friend go off in a hailed down carriage. His thoughts were hardened, and he felt nothing would change his mind from his early unspoken decision. *He was content with his current* life, he thought. *Why break the silence in his* heart?

Wednesday was a short a day for Gabe. He made early rounds at the hospital. Next, he would go to the office and stay until about 1:00. After that, the office was closed, and he planned to make a couple of visits to patients at their home who couldn't make it to the office. He had just finished at the Lester's house, which was an apartment above the hardware store. He had made it to his carriage when he heard some voices that made him stop.

"Miss Belle seems like you insulted the Captain here. You know you could be arrested for insulting an officer."

"Let me alone, sir. You are blocking my way."

The man grabbed for the packages the miss was holding and ripped open the boxes.

"What do we have here, a fancy dress to dance at one of those fancy parties? It seems a shame to be worn like a trash heap from Savannah, don't you think Saul, when so many of our buddies came home mangled like our friend Baxter? It's just not right. Fancy dances and pretty dresses while men are bleeding and get hacked to pieces by bayonets. The man took a knife from his pocket and made cuts into the dress while another man held the woman's hands behind her back and covered her mouth. "Just like that," and the predator took another slash at the dress.

Gabriel came from around the carriage and took a horsewhip. He snapped the knife out of the hands of the perpetrator and then kicked it under the carriage. He then turned and snapped the whip between the two men with evil on their mind who meant to torment the young miss. With a furry in his eye. Gabriel growled at the males standing in shock. "Get out of my sight right now or risk a loss of a limb! I may not be left standing when this is over, but by God, you will know that you have tangled with Major Hamilton in defending the innocent over your despicable souls."

The largest of the ruffians stepped back and assessed the situation. Though there were more of them, Gabriel struck the cord of fear in both of the ruffians. "Let's go boys, we mean no trouble with the Major. We were just having a little fun" All three men separated and ran back to an alley between the shops.

By this time, an older man came down the street with boxes in his hand. He came closer to the lass. "Miss Sofie, what has happened?"

She looked back in tears at the older man and said, "It's okay, George. It's all over now."

By this time, Gabriel had gone under the carriage to pick up the knife and handed it to the man who came to meet the young women.

"Your uncle would kill me if I let anything happen to you, Miss Sofie. Your father would then feed my carcass to the sharks."

Sofie looked up at the older man with empathy and respect for the dear English butler who had been with the family for years. "It's all alright now. We can go home now, can't we?" the young lady said with sniffles. "I seemed to have messed up this day already. You are late because you were doing what I asked, all because I wanted to pick up my dress early to show my friends. It was selfish of me, and I learned my lesson. I'm sorry George, but I think I must return home now. I must brace up to my aunt's and uncle's scolding, if they receive wind of what's happened. My aunt will surely be upset over the dress."

"Yes miss. Let me put his in the carriage." George put his packages in the carriage and then went to grab the boxes that Sofie had picked off the ground."

"Oh my, what has happened? Did someone try to steal these packages from you, miss?"

A male voice interjected. "No, the young lady was stopped by three fellows of bad intentions and when she tried to avoid them, the boxes were opened, and the contents were damaged. I chased them off. I will give you this knife for safekeeping. This belonged to the fellow I struck first," said Gabriel. My name is Dr. Gabriel Hamilton. I watched what happened from my carriage over there. Are you, sir, the young lady's father?"

"Oh no, sir, Miss Sofie Van Doran is staying with her uncle. Her father is Admiral Rodger Van Doran."

"Thank you, George. I can speak for myself. I am Sofie Van Doran, Dr. Gabriel Hamilton. I give you my sincerest thank you for helping me with those ruffians."

Gabriel looked into the eyes of the young women. "Miss Van Dorn, for you, I believe I would have protected you with my life if necessary. Are you far from home? May I escort you to your door?"

Sofie blushed and smiled back. "Thank you, sir. I will be fine. Your words, I believe, are sincere." If we may, I would like George to take me home now. My family will be worried about us if we tarry much longer. Perhaps our paths will cross again."

Gabriel smiled back. "Yes, perhaps they will cross indeed on a much happier occasion."

Gabriel helped the young lady into her carriage. He then went to his own and unlashed the horses. In his mind, a thought came to him. *I have plans for* Saturday, *after all. How fortunate to meet a Van Dorn who will be most interesting to get to know a little better.* Gabriel watched the carriage drive off and followed from a distance, making sure its occupants made it home safely.

Later that evening, Gabriel sat in his small library reading through his most recent mail, visitor cards left, and invitations that had arrived during the week. *How interesting! There was an embossed envelope with an invitation. The invite used* a Rose Lane. It stated that a party would be held at the Van Dorns in honor of the recent return of Admiral Rodger Van Dorn from his recent military service. Yes, the addresses matched where the carriage had stopped. Gabriel knew he would send a message to James and his wife in the morning with his change of mind. He would very much enjoy going with them on Saturday night, after all.

Chapter 14

Dinner Guest

S aturday had arrived. The carriages were already in a line
by 7:30 PM. After being introduced at the front door and
greeted by the hostess and host, the invites migrated between
the two front parlors which were opened up for the evening for
extra room. Luckily enough, the dinner party was for approximately twenty guests, which suited the space and the ability for
the dinner to remain intimate among the guests. Gabriel was
introduced to the other quests gathering in the front parlors.
Fortunately, he was acquainted with many of them in atten-
dance. He searched the adjoining rooms whenever he had the
chance to see if Sofie was present. Nearing the time for the
call to move to the dining room. A lavender silk with silver
slippers appeared on the stairs. She continued downward and

a middle-aged man came from another room to meet her as she made her last step.

"Father, she blurted out with joy on her face and her hands out reached." The room was lit up with sounds of appreciation and the room.

"Rodger, you've stolen the child's grand entrance!" the hostess said with laughter.

"Can't a father bring his daughter to the dining table?"

"No, he can't." Mrs. Van Dorn responded and walked over to her brother-in-law and his daughter. She gave a kiss on the cheek to the guest of honor. She was delighted to add, "Welcome home!"

The Admiral blushed, smiled, and bowed low to his hostess. He looked quietly over the all guests. "Ahh, Milli. I've just arrived all cleaned and dressed like a peacock. I hope this makes you happy. I would do this for no one else," Rodger replied.

"You have perfect timing. I was just talking with the cook, who stated that dinner was ready to be served. I have a lovely lady I want you to escort to dinner. It's not proper for you to escort your daughter to dinner this evening. I believe you know Mrs. Anderson."

"That I do, Milli." Rodger said with a wink. "A lovely choice indeed." Rodger, playing the part of a gentleman, walked toward the recently widowed Mrs. Anderson. "Mrs. Anderson, would you grace me with your lovely presence? My sister-in-law is forbidding me to escort my daughter to my party. But I have the honor of asking you to sit beside me and brighten my evening!"

"Admiral Van Dorn, it would be my honor," said Mrs. Anderson will all smiles. "I must request a promise that you will be a perfect gentleman."

"My dear, you have always been safe when you have been with me. I am just bewitched by your beauty as ever." Both partners had sparkles in their eyes that showed they had secrets between them.

"Sofie, darling, now that you have joined us. I want to introduce you to some guests that I believe you will enjoy speaking with. Mrs. Van Dorn was careful to introduce her niece to specific guests and telling her a little of each one. By the time Sofie stood in front of the McDaniels and Dr. Hamilton, it was time to call for dinner. How convenient it was for the hostess to join her niece and Dr. Hamilton as a pair around the formal dining table. Dr. Hamilton knew this was how things were done in society. Typically, it was the very thing he avoided at such social get togethers. However, Mrs. Van Dorn was as graceful as a ballerina. Lovely as she was, Sofie showed even brighter. He suspected that the dress was borrowed from Sofie's aunt, as it had the sophistication of someone who had dressed for society before. *It was stunning.*

"Dr. Hamilton, I believe I can count on you to be a perfect gentleman escorting Sofie. She told me of your gallant intervention the other day. We are ever so thankful for your assistance. Sofie, I believe you can keep your *father from corrupting Dr.*

Hamilton at dinner before he even gets to know us," said Mrs. Van Dorn with a warm smile.

"Yes, Aunt Milli," Sofie responded, knowing the underlying meaning of her words. She sent a charming smile to Dr. Hamilton.

Other guests filed in and filled the dining room with laughter and murmuring conversations. Witty responses and jovial tails flowed through the courses as excellent aged wine from the finest of vineyards. This was obviously a group of people who enjoyed these gatherings. Gabriel did not experience the stuffy discussions that were had at many soirees. This was something that he had missed in his life recently, even though he had attended many events and dinners. He looked around and liked the people he was with. They had a common bond. Sofie was witty and charming. Her speech was just as southern as sweet tea on the front veranda. She spoke French as smooth as Irish whiskey. Her complexion was of the Danish blood line. Her cultured ways were from the French inspired finishing school she attended. Gabrial admired the results. But there was something more. She had something on the inside that drew one in. How did those ruffians even want to humiliate this diamond? It made Gabrial mad and sad. Didn't they know who she was? No, they couldn't have been that evil. It was their ignorance, Gabriel thought. She shined brighter than anyone at the table. Those fellows couldn't see it because they were not made from the same substance. Gabriel's impression of Admiral Van Dorn was the opposite of delicate. His stories were intoxicating to the ears of the guests. A union officer from the coastal south, which was an interesting mixture during the war. The Van Dorn's were an interesting family. He was already under their spell.

After about two hours of dinner and then conversation, Gabriel quietly walked outside on the terrace after dinner, attempting to get some space between the lovely young ladies inside.

"So, Dr. Hamilton, it's good to see that you made it home from the war safely. God must want to protect you for a bigger purpose." The voice from the other side of the porch had a twang. It was part southern, but also spicier, like someone from the Caribbean or New Orleans.

"Yes, so it would seem. It's just taking some time to put the pieces since I've been out of the military."

"Have you thought of moving from academia to be part of the medical officers planning the growing network of veteran's infirmaries?"

"You know, I hadn't really thought about that. I had spoken with some men on the academic at the academy . But I didn't feel the connection."

"Well, there are others who could really use your medical skills. I might have some connections. We need good men who are good at administration and have the clinical knowledge that the people deserve. The Civil War has brought men home in mangled conditions. There are many opportunities out there. They are talking about a medical support system for our veterans in Washington. It is in the early stages. I suspect you have been visiting with some chaps in New England and in your home state."

"I had some time working on the first hospital trains when I was in Georgia. I later worked with the pavilion style hospitals that were before I left the service," said Gabriel. "I really felt needed while I was in the Army."

"Finding one's purpose is an important thing to consider. The daily decisions about how to invest time and energy are an ever cross for most men of importance," Admiral Van Dorn responded. "I will keep my eyes and ears open for you, but I think you will find your niche very soon. On another note, I heard you ran into some young men that wanted to have some fun at my daughter's expense this week. I thank you for intervening."

"They were just wicked men, wanting to hurt an innocent for their fun," said Gabriel.

"I want you to know they are in the brig as we speak."

"How did you know?" Gabriel asked.

"I keep a tight watch on my daughter. Someone would have intervened on my orders. You were quicker than them and I am very obliged. I appreciate your concern for my daughter's welfare," said Sofie's father.

"Your daughter is a treasure. I'm sure you are aware of that. Sir, I have just met her and yet she shines greater than gold coins or gems." Gabriel said in earnest.

"Well doctor, you seem to have knowledge more than other men I know. The influence of her aunt and uncle has refined her, but she still has her mother's passion for life. I wished I had been around her more as she grew up. I tried to do my best by her after her mother died."

Gabriel's intrigue was growing. "I assume you are an admiral for the Union. Did you see much activity?"

"Yes, I saw some regarding protecting the cargo and those aboard, but I was more interested in the supply aspects. I am a builder of boats, Gabriel. My title is more of an honorary title than one earned from action. When you bring your own small ships to the president and ask how can you serve, you are given a title to run and use those ships for military purposes. I had some hospital ships on the coast and others down the Mississippi. We moved supplies and soldiers. What I didn't use my ships for was firing on people or property. I drew the line on fighting. Only to protect my crew would I fire on another ship.

"It sounds like you were in a unique position." Gabriel responded.

"Perhaps. I made a promise about how I try to live my life. That forms my choices. However, I will admit there were times, the choices I had were not ones I wanted to take. But I had to choose. That was true in war and in life. Did you ever fire on a man during the war?"

"My role was to heal people, not fight," said Gabriel.

"I see. So you know the conflict when you're pushed by others to make decisions that you don't want to make. That is where the real conflict starts. I have found that to prepare for making that decision at the right time in battle, I needed to prepare my heart long before the battle started."

"Are you a philosophical sailor, Admiral?" Gabriel asked

"No, I'm very practical. I can't go through the fighting and chaos in this world without a leader in me to guide me. My fear is that I might come to a situation where I wasn't prepared. I'm not a perfect man, Gabriel. But I've seen where I could have fallen on my sword, and many times I should have."

Gabriel listened intently. "Is this what you taught your daughter?"

"No, her mother taught her the real lessons in life. She taught her to understand what love is and how to give and receive. I couldn't do that. I wouldn't know how to begin. Sofie has that special thing that knows how to love deeply and strongly. She's young yet, but I see it in her just like I saw it in her mother. Do I see it in other women? Yes, I do, but not all women are to be my wife or my partner. I respect the emotion and honor it for the treasure that it is, but it does not belong to me. I think a man once named David should have understood this sage advice, but he somehow missed this lesson from the great maestro who taught him to play the harp and write poetry. Do you know I love poetry Dr. Hamilton? It soothes my nerves when the gales are building. And when the tempest is at its peak, I sing the songs of old. The ones written from the soul of a man during times of highs and lows. Yes, I seek comfort too in the darkness of the night as when the howling of the wind is searching to devour myself and the crew. I sing quietly inside my heart. That doesn't sound like a warrior's heart, does it? But I am that kind of man. I have found no other way to quiet my world. I must be boring you. This old man makes no sense. I just rambled because of too much wine at the table this evening."

"It makes a lot of sense, Admiral. I have nothing to judge you. It would not be my role, anyway. I'm just a man. I don't pride myself on being the smartest or most successful. Believe me, my background is a checkered as gingham." A little embarrassed, Gabriel went on. "I've just met your daughter. Yet I'm already feeling something that you described. I'm not sure I should be asking you this so soon, but I want to be with her for the rest of my days. I am embarrassed to tell you because I don't understand it myself."

The admiral chuckled. "You're the fourth one who has asked for Sofie's hand in marriage today, but I think you're the only one who I believe. I suspected so much when I saw your carcass being thrown around in a tavern outside of Washington with your companions in crime three years ago. You were drunk to almost a stupor. Had I not intervened, I'm sure your nose would not be as fine as it is today. I also suspect your hands would not be able to cut into flesh with a straight line with that scalpel you use either. Such a loss of talent for a just a few pints of cheap tavern whiskey. Yes, life has its humor, doesn't Dr. Hamilton?" The elder man started to walk away and turned before he walked back into the parlor. "We'll see what my daughter has to say about all this. She's learning to use discernment like her mother. Perhaps she sees what I could never see. Why would any woman love a creature as pitiful as a man I will never understand? It's all in there, you know, the black book that came in your aunt's care box. Your Aunt Arline has been praying over you for a long time, Gabriel. She was a fine young lady when I was a cadet. She was not the one for me, Gabriel. I was an impatient, hot-tempered son of a carpenter who had made his living making boats. I ran off to the sea. I heard her prayers many times since I left that village watching over me. I heard her prayers that night in that tavern watching over you. I honored her request. She was always my choice, but the God above gave me another chance at the right time, who loved me deeper and richer, and I am ever so grateful. The admiral patted Gabriel on the back and went inside.

Gabriel was left on the patio in amazement. *What is happening to me? Did the Admiral just say something that connected him with a secret of his past?* The care boxes came on a schooner when he was at the field hospital outside of Richmond. "Wow!" Gabriel spoke out loud. *I came this evening on a lark after meeting a damsel in the street. I covered her back with my protection in a moment of time. I never knew it would lead to this.* He took a deep breath before entering the house again. He could hear someone playing on the piano in the front room. It was a French folk tune. Gabriel remembered the song from his studies in the classic languages. He went inside and joined the others. The sweet sound wafting from a music room pushed out the cobwebs and skeletons in his memory. He looked around the library after he closed the door behind him and noted one man missing from the room. Where did that sly admiral go? Gabriel thought for a moment and wondered if the ladies were missing anyone in the parlor. Gabriel ventured towards his friend Mc-Daniel, needing an anchor that was strong enough to hold him wandering aimlessly.

"Gabriel, is everything okay? We haven't seen you mixing with any of the young ladies. We thought that would be good for you."

"It's all fine. I am surprised to have lost in a game of chance by an expert player, and I didn't even know I was in the game."

"Do you want to talk about it?" Mc Daniel asked.

"No, I don't, but I have a favor to ask." He patted Mc-Daniels's back and walked away. The night would end soon, and Gabriel's life would take a new turn as it had in Georgia, away from Dunbar's Gap.

Chapter 15

The Admiral's Daughter

For the next two weeks, Gabriel visited the Van Dorn home. He filled himself with the tidbits he was learning about this young lady. She expressed the southern belle softness but also had a gritty quality of salt of the sea. Perhaps that was her father's contribution to her being. He found her even more a mystery when she surrounded herself with accomplishments with an assortment of skills, not just the womanly skills one would learn at a finishing school. She knew how to tie a sailor's knot and carve a figurine from soft pine as good as any seasoned sailor. Sofie understood the constellations in the sky. Taking tea with her and her family was like walking through a library, but the books were the people who could recite passages and recall details from the dusty pages. By the end of the second week,

Gabriel had spoken with Sofie about his conversation with her father and requested her hand for marriage. Sofie showed no resistance to the match. Indeed, she was quite happy. However, not all were as pleased with the match for many ladies who frequented the social circle as the Van Dorns had wondered how the southern bell had cast her net on the most prominent bachelor in town in so short of time.

Six weeks later, in a chapel that looked upon a garden along the river near Gabriel's boyhood home, people had gathered. Sofie's aunt and uncle sat beside the admiral on the first church pew. Gabriel's father and mother sat on the other side of the aisle. The friends and family sat behind the pews marked with garden flowers brought by two ladies. Gabriel had met them privately while they were at work. He had heard them singing through the window and instantly recognized the song. He had heard it while he was leaving the gap between the soldiers and the wagon of two women. Dr. Hamilton had heard the song again in the voice of fever by the confused patient at the Thaxtons' home. Gabriel thanked the lovely ladies for the kindness they showed on this special day. He asked about their welfare and invited them to stay, but only if they would sing. And so there was music at the church that day. The guests welcomed the new Mr. and Mrs. Gabriel Thaxton's. Men weren't supposed to cry, but Dr. Hamilton cried when he saw their faces as they took the seat behind the piano. He sniffled back more tears as he saw the smiling faces of Lacey and her husband. *They had all been there in the gap in one form or* another, *whether in spirit or flesh. John, who saw me in the darkest times. As he walked with me past the tables of bloodied men and screams, he didn't flinch outwardly. He said he was a coward. No, Gabriel knew better. Cowards don't walk away when one sees war. They sometimes fall on their knees and that makes the difference. Even in Gabriel's rebellious ways, far from where he grew up and the parents who loved him, someone was looking after him and steering him home.* He realized that now.

Sofie's father sat intently, listening to the harmonizing voices. It was like he was on his schooner again up the river, walking along the deck as if he was a young man again. He visualized his wife's face. Her countenance glowed the first time he saw her in the moonlight twenty years ago. Gigi's face sealed the purpose of Sofie's father for life. As he sat on the pew, he thought silently. *That young man that I crossed in* Washington *has grown so much. He never saw me in that tavern filled* with *sailors and riffraff. I protected him as best I could.*

Sofie placed her hand in her husband's and allowed Gabriel to take her to the carriage that was waiting. "Mr. Hamilton, I believe it is time for us to leave."

Gabriel looked at his beautiful wife with her golden hair spirals along her face. Gabriel fell out of the trance when he heard a booming voice come up on a carriage beside him. "It's your time, sir. We've got to make the ship while the tide is still high. We will meet the ocean by morning."

Gabriel smiled back at his father-in-law. "We'll be ready." For the next 8 weeks, Gabriel committed himself to the whims of the admiral on a southern voyage along the coast. The final destination was Savannah, Sofie's childhood home. On the first day at sea, Gabriel looked at the man at the helm. He laughed and looked at Sofie. "Is your father a real admiral?" Gabriel asked.

Sofie laughed with a twinkle in her eye. "Yes!" In his mind, he rides the seas as a captain for the admiral who can only be seen by those who believe.

"Sounds like a prophet from the Bible," Gabriel responded.

"You've met my father; does he seem like a prophet to you?" Sofie responded with a laugh.

"Well, I'm not one to judge and I can't say I ever met a prophet in person, but he listens to things other than what seems obvious."

"Wait till you get to know him more. He has a reason for everything he does. Even his spontaneous trips or walks in the park at unpredictable times of the day have a reason."

"See, that's what I mean. He doesn't do what others expect." Gabriel too took a second to look up at the admiral on his own sailing vessel. The man and his ship looked totally occupied. Gabriel looked at Sofie and asked. "If I made a surprising decision, would you agree with it?"

"Perhaps, I'm not sure? Is this a challenge right at the beginning of our marriage?"

"I have friends Sofie, who will work with me on this. I know they will. I want to build a system of hospitals for the care of soldiers. I want to make it a research community too. There could be a network of care facilities where young men can be trained and given the best tools for their craft. I met a man on the train from New York. He and his sons are building a unique and inspiring hospital out west. I want to be inspired by his motivation to do the best he can do for his patients. Sofie, I feel on fire for what I want to do with my skills. I want you to be a part of that too, but are you willing to go with me on this crazy journey?"

Sofie had tears in her eyes. "Yes, Gabriel. I've been waiting for a long time for you to come home. The Dubar Gap seems like a dreary place. It reminds me of a place where an injured child, son of a prince, once lived with no hope of being rescued or cared for. It's in the Bible?"

"How did you know about Dunbar Gap?" Gabriel asked incredulously. I didn't think I had ever spoken to you about that time in my life." Gabriel was in amazement of this surprise revelation.

Before Sofie could say anything more, her father cried out. *"Come and take a look at this? Hurry!" called out the Admiral.*

Gabriel sighed with frustration. For now, Gabriel would have to wait for an answer.

Sofie thought the secret would need to remain forever unknown. In her heart, she suspected no one would ever know the full secret of the courier on Dunbar's Gap. The rider low in the saddle traveling through lost passages would never be entirely known. The full secret would never be revealed because no one had all the pieces.

The Admiral, with his wisdom, had successfully distracted his son-in-law from his conversation below. "Now would you look at that, Gabriel? I see land with the lighthouse already starting to glow. Take a look through my eye piece," the admiral cried out. "It looks like a candle to any sailor welcoming them home."

Sofie pulled Gabriel by the hand to follow her to the helm. Her face lit up like a halo in the sun upon the deck. Gabriel's wife's bonnet tossed to her back, hanging by silk ribbons. Her long tresses whipped around her head from the winds.

"I see why you love her," Gabriel announced as he took the eye piece and peered to the south.

"Yes indeed, mate. We are lucky to be blessed by the good women of the world and destroyed by the bad ones who try to counterfeit the good ones." The admiral looked out over the body of water between the schooner and the shore. "The love of my youth is there. No matter where I go, she comes with me as long as I promise to bring her back home."

"Rodger, is Savannah your home?"

Sofie's father looked more intent with a squint in his eye as he continued to watch the sea. "My home is where I am called. Sometimes I am planting palms in the garden on Ballast street, or other times I am sitting at a tavern outside of Washington. I might even be on the Mississippi, bringing supplies up the river. Wherever I am, I am certainly not alone. To add to your question, you've never been alone either, Gabriel. No matter how lonely it was for you up the highlands, someone knew you were there."

"I believe my father is telling of his adventurous life. It is difficult to tell between his fabulous tales and his monstrous lies." Sofie chimed in and wrapped her arms around her husband.

"I see. Which ones do you think I should believe?" Gabriel asked in jest."

"I say it's all or nothing!" Sofie laughed. "You can believe everything he says, and you will sometimes be right. You can believe nothing he says, and you will be wrong sometimes. If you pick and choose what he says is true or false, you could be wrong entirely by missing the truth."

"Incredible logical, my girl." The admiral laughed.

Chapter 16

Hard Candy

In two more days, the schooner moored at the harbor in Savannah. Military activity continued, but at least supplies were trickling in. Savannah was grossly intact from Sherman's occupation. A wharf full of activity along the river was observed as the schooner pulled near the docks. Gabriel heard the church bells ringing before the boat had reached the area where the cotton exchange was in view. Upon arrival, there was unloading to be arranged. The admiral took off after securing a private carriage for his daughter and his son-in-law. They would go on to 10 Ballast Street, several blocks from the wharf, and open Sofie's childhood home with free liberation. A wagon of goods would follow behind so that the family would not be in immediate need. The idea was not to prepare for a long duration, but only to settle for a month. Sofie could select what she wanted for her new home near Gabriel's office. Her father would arrange for things to be shipped by boat. It was likely that the Admiral would sell the home, as his needs were different now that the war had ended. The admiral hadn't spoken on the matter, but the decision seemed logical. The admiral himself had business to take care, so he left Sofie and Gabriel to go to the home and start unpacking immediately needed items. They would not have the help of a housemaid on this trip, but they should find things in good order. The admiral typically left things very livable between visits. Within the next two days, Sofie was asked to tag all the things that she wished to send north. Things that could be purchased near her new home or did not have sentimental value would most likely be sold off.

The Admiral was deciding on how to get supplies from his small warehouse to liquidate the items he stored for missions. A contraband hospital in a location close with easy access to water would be a good choice. He had a contact there, and he knew a woman could be trusted to distribute the supplies where most needed sticking to his rules of anonymity. Most of his ship building equipment was moved or sold at the time the war broke out. Given his loyalties, he had not wanted to be in a compromising position should the confederacy knock on his door. The Admiral knew the schooners were no longer the vessels of choice with the invention of steam engines and mechanization, so there was no reason to reinvest time and money in rebuilding the business in shipbuilding. The Admiral stopped in to speak with his solicitor and completed some transactions. He had one more thing he wanted to do before he returned to Ballast Street. It was his private time with Gigi. Now that was starting a new chapter in his life, the admiral wanted to tell Gigi everything. His private moments at her grave gave him the confidence to make his next moves.

****]

Gabriel had helped with carrying, opening, and pulling things down from high places. At this point in the evening, sweat rolled from his forehead and arms. He sat on the steps with rolled up cuffs wiping his brow with a damp cloth. "Your father and mother must have been very happy here."

"Yes, we were all happy here. The springtime in this city is beautiful. Each home on this street had a garden in the back. Of course, there was an herb garden, but there was always room for a cut flower garden. My mother loved the smell of gardenias. When you sit on the back porch in the evenings, you can smell the fragrance. Camelias bloom in the winter months. It makes me happy to see the color when nothing else is blooming. I never saw my parents fight. Sometimes they disagreed about things, but they didn't fight about their differences. My father could get spices rather easily and my mother was the only woman at church who had a large marble cutting board. Around Christmas, all the ladies would come over for the day and make hard tack candy. There was peppermint, cinnamon, cloves and probably some other flavors I don't recall. The mothers would put the young children in a safe place and the older children's job was filling the candy bags once it cooled. It was one of the fondest memories I can recall with my mother."

"So how did your mother make it to the colonies?" Gabe asked.

"She was from a French family living in Canada. Her grandfather was a fur trader. Things were happening with the invasion of the English. They came to the states because they felt it might have more opportunities. My mother was a dressmaker helping her mother in a shop near your hometown. My father accompanied his mother and sisters to the shop. I guess my father liked the dresses very much, and he married the dressmaker's daughter. There was a fuss at first, I'm sure, but eventually my father's family accepted the marriage. That's how I became friends with Mrs. Jennings and Lacey Thaxton. Lacey and I went to finishing school together, but she is a couple of years older."

"I don't think you told me that before," said Gabriel. He smiled with understanding and tugged on one of her spirals.

"My mother died when she was twenty-seven from pneumonia. It broke my father's heart. He has always had a soft spot for the forsaken and downtrodden. I'm not sure why. I'm not aware of all that he has witnessed to make him sensitive to that, but it's there."

"Your father appears to be an interesting man. I think I like him very much, but he is rather mysterious. Okay, I think I have cooled off now. Lead me to the next room and tell me what is next."

"Let's hit the nursery. It's the room between my parents' room and my old room. Nobody has used that room for years. I would like to see if there are some things left that I would like to save."

After thirty minutes of picking some trunks and furniture that Sofia wanted to keep.

Gabriel stopped to look around. "This room has been used lately and more frequently than you think."

"Why do you say that?"

"It's not very dusty." Gabriel commented. "Housekeepers did not n't dust homes if they are note visited. Rooms are ignored if they are not being used. This home has the signs that both have been happening."

"Okay, I understand your point. Perhaps my father had a guest staying that we are not aware of. This would normally not be a room a guest would use. My father could have traveled to Savannah and stayed a night or two, but he wouldn't have dusted this room. He wouldn't have come into this room unless he had kept something in here that he wanted to get."

"I agree. Sofia, I'm not sure what we'll find here. Do you want to keep looking in here? My hunch is we have found evidence of what your father has been up to the last four years, perhaps even longer."

"I'm not afraid of my father's actions. I would also like to keep some pieces in here. I like that chest over there. You can open it."

"Okay," Gabriel responded. The first two drawers had books and a pouch. I'm going to open this leather pouch that's at the bottom of this chest. Fifteen minutes later, Gabriel was still reading the log entries in a journal. Most of the information had been coded in numbers with some letters or words after indicating a systematic journal for inventory. Eventually he came to entries with two locations, the first being Dunbar Mill and the second being Dunbar Gap. Gabriel looked at the dates. They corresponded with time the start time of when the soldiers arrived for encampment and when they left to meet the column. Various entries recorded with specific notes grabbing Gabriel's close attention. One entry had been for the night before the group and left the gap. The night of the missing items from camp was noted. Different initials were recorded. The next day, another code was used noted with two items transferred by wagon. Gabriel was sure of the two items transferred by wagon on that day. He was there. Other notations followed. Gabriel couldn't make out the codes or locations on many of the other entries.

"I see you found something in here of your interest." The male voice was came from the doorway to the room.

Gabriel turned to see his father-in-law standing there, looking back. "I'm not sure what I am looking at, but I recognize a few entries and assume what their purpose of the entries was about."

"What do you think you understand?" said Admiral Van Dorn.

"Logs of supplies delivered; things transferred all in code. I assume this is all yours?"

"Perhaps."

"What does it all mean?" Gabriel asked.

"I can't say. I kept logs in case someone questioned activities."

"I am questioning?"

"Son, we never had this conversation?"

"I'm hearing that phrase a bit too often. What does it mean?"

"Gabriell, I distributed supplies and transported people in the war. Sometimes I could get messages through when no one else could. Things you saw were not the same for me. I didn't always get the entire picture of my missions."

"Did I get special treatment?'

"I can't answer that. I was told to keep you well supplied. From what I understand, your medical unit far outperformed many of the other units. That's why you ended up in Washington the second time. They needed you. The military had a few surgeons with your expertise, but they weren't everywhere. Grant was carrying a lot of casualties on his shoulders. He needed you in his campaigns."

"Why the courier?"

"I'm not at liberty to discuss the courier. That was managed by someone, but higher than me."

"Who can be higher than an admiral?" Gabriel asked in exasperation. Then Gabriel whispered only a few men are that powerful and one of them is gone.

The admiral stood in silence. "Gabriel, may I have those logs back?" Gabriel slowly gave them back. His father-in-law lit a match and began burning the logs in the fireplace. "We never had this conversation," the admiral stated for a second time.

Gabriel spent the rest of the night glueing the pieces together from events of the last 5 years of his life. By the time he had gone to bed, Sofia was fast asleep. He couldn't bother her now to explain what he was feeling. Perhaps in the morning it wouldn't matter so much. He looked up at the ceiling for another hour or two just thinking of all heaviness of that had passed. Yet there were these moments that had brought him simple pleasures to be alive. Pepper, his horse, was waiting for him back at his father's farm. Gabriel missed having Pepper to ride out to countryside and back. He wanted to allow the horse to run free. He also missed the taste of hot coffee on a brisk morning. His mother knitted socks that felt so soft on cold, tired, aching feet. Gabriel smiled in the darkness. He received a surprise in one of the courier's packages at Christmas. He remembered it so clearly: the fragrance of orange and cloves bursting out of the tin, infusing the air with the most heavenly sent. Someone had made hard tack candy. Gabriel looked at the diminutive creature beside him. Could it have come from this kitchen and from Sofie's hands? He couldn't believe that it was true, but in the realm of possibilities, it had a chance to be true. Gabriel remembered what she had said about her father's tales. Perhaps he dared to believe them. Even if events as told were not totally true, he had a chance that parts of his story was true, just like the tales of the admiral. His life was like a weaver's cloth; each thread was part of a larger design. Somewhere between hard tack candy and the use of bromine for the care of wounds, Gabriel's thoughts swirled. He had pursued finding the truth about the courier of Dunbar Gap. Along the way he was creating his own tale that would be told by likes of the bearded men at the corner pub or left in a box with mementos of the war in a dusty attic. With a new chapter to begin in the morning, Gabriel finally fell off to sleep in peace.

About the author

D.L. Barnes lives near Atlanta, Georgia. The author's love for the natural beauty of the Appalachian mountains inspired a tale of goodness of the heart.

Other books by the author

Salty Beginnings

Burning Bush Bakery

Captain Bodacious

Recent release

The Courier of Dunbar Gap

Acknowledgements

The author would like to acknowledge the resources that were part of the inspiration and preparation for this book.

Kennesaw National Battlefield Park, Kennesaw, Georgia

Chickamauga and Chattanooga National Military Park, Fort Oglethorpe, Georgia

Appomattox Court House National Historical Park, Appomattox, Virginia

Resaca National Battlefield Historical site, Resaca, Georgia

Booth Western Museum, Cartersville, Georgia

Cold Harbor Battlefield, Mechanicsville, VA